# FAVORITE Fairy Tales

# FAVORITE Fairy Tales

## Edited by Diana Bremer

CHARTWELL BOOKS INC.

*Acknowledgment*

The publishers appreciate the co-operation of Mr Baum's estate in
allowing them retell *Dorothy and the Witch* from THE WIZARD OF OZ

This edition first published in the USA by Chartwell Books Inc.
a division of Book Sales, Inc., 110 Enterprise Avenue, Secaucus, New Jersey 07094

Text © 1974 Octopus Books Limited.
Illustrations © 1974 L'Esperto S.p.A., Milan-Octopus Books Limited, London

ISBN 0 7064 0632 X

Produced and printed by Mandarin Publishers Limited
22A Westlands Road, Quarry Bay, Hong Kong

# Contents

# The Gingerbread Man

ONCE upon a time there was an old man and an old woman and a little boy. One day the woman made a Gingerbread Man and put it in the oven to bake. She said to the little boy, "Your father and I are going out to work in the fields. Keep an eye on the Gingerbread Man."

Suddenly the little boy saw the oven door burst open and out jumped the Gingerbread Man and ran off down the garden path. The boy chased after him, shouting, "The Gingerbread Man is running away! Help! Help!" The old man and the old woman threw down their tools and joined in the chase. But the Gingerbread Man shouted back, "Run! Run! As fast as you can! You can't catch me, I'm the Gingerbread Man!"

Next three mowers in a field called out, "Where are you going, Gingerbread Man?"

"I've outrun an old man and an old woman and a little boy," he replied, "and I can outrun you too!"

"You can, can you?" cried the mowers, and they started to run after him. "Run!

Run!" laughed the Gingerbread Man, "as fast as you can! You can't catch me, I'm the Gingerbread Man!" And he ran so fast that he soon disappeared and the mowers flopped down exhausted under a tree.

On ran the Gingerbread Man, and presently he came across a brown bear lying in the sand. "Where are you going to, Gingerbread Man?" the bear asked.

"I've outrun an old man and an old woman and a little boy and three mowers, and I can outrun you *too*," he replied.

"You can, can you?" growled the bear, and began to chase after him. "Run! Run!" laughed the Gingerbread Man, "as fast as you can! You can't catch me, I'm the Gingerbread Man!" And he ran so fast that he left the bear far behind him.

After a while he came across a fox curled up under some bushes by the roadside. "Where are you running to?" called the fox.

"I've outrun an old man and an old woman and a little boy and three mowers and a bear," he hollered back, "and I'm

quite sure that I can outrun you *too.*"

The fox whispered, "I can't hear you. Come closer." So the Gingerbread Man went closer and shouted, "*I've outrun an old man and an old woman and a little boy and three mowers and a bear, and I can outrun you too!*"

"You can, can you?" smiled the fox, and snapped him up and swallowed him whole. And that was the end of the poor boastful Gingerbread Man.

# Goldilocks & the Three Bears

Once there was a pretty little girl who was called Goldilocks because her head was covered in golden curls. She liked to walk by herself in the woods; when she was hungry she would eat the wild strawberries there, and when she was tired she would sleep on the dry moss.

Three bears lived in the woods: Father

Bear, who was big and had a deep voice, and Mother Bear, who was smaller and rounder and had a middling-deep voice, and Baby Bear, who was like a ball of fur and had a squeaky voice. Because they were all such different sizes, each one of them had his own chair, own bed and own porridge bowl.

Every evening Mother Bear used to put the porridge to soak in a saucepan on the oven, and every morning she boiled it up and poured it into the three bowls for the bears' breakfast. On the morning that this story happened, the sun was shining in the window and the birds were singing outside, and Father Bear and Baby Bear were splashing around in the stream behind the house, having their morning wash. Mother Bear called to them that breakfast was ready, and they all sat down in front of their bowls of steaming hot porridge.

"Oh! My porridge is too hot!" exclaimed Father Bear in his deep, gruff voice.

"Oh! My porridge is too hot too!" said Mother Bear in her softer voice.

"Oh! My porridge is too hot too!" said Baby Bear in his squeaky voice.

So they all decided to go out for a walk until their porridge had cooled down. No sooner had they left their cottage than Goldilocks came along. She was hungry and tired because she had been walking for a long time, and she decided to stop for a while at this strange little cottage.

She looked in through the window and saw a well-scrubbed wooden table with three bowls of porridge laid out on it, and around it three chairs to sit on. "Is anybody home?" she called out, but nobody answered her. The bears had left the door ajar, so Goldilocks walked through the door into the bears' living room. Since there was no one there she sat down in Father Bear's chair to rest. But it was much too big for her, and her feet could not even reach the ground. So she climbed down and into Mother Bear's chair, and wriggled around in it to get comfortable. In the end she decided that it was too big for her too, so she hopped off and sat down in Baby Bear's chair which broke because it was too small.

Goldilocks walked around the table again, and the smell of the porridge made her hungry. She dipped a spoon into Father Bear's bowl, but the porridge in it was too hot, and she dropped it again. Then she tried some from Mother Bear's bowl, but that was too cold. The porridge in Baby Bear's bowl was just right, and Goldilocks ate it all up.

By now she was very sleepy, and when

she caught sight of a large bed in the next room she decided she would have a short rest before returning home. So she climbed up into Father Bear's bed, but when she lay down on it, it was so big that she felt quite uncomfortable. So she climbed off it quickly and went to lie in Mother Bear's bed. But that one was so soft that she still felt quite uncomfortable, so she scrambled out of it again quickly. Then she tried Baby Bear's bed, which was so comfortable that she immediately fell fast asleep.

Soon afterwards the three bears returned. "Somebody's been eating my porridge!" Father Bear thundered when he saw the wooden spoon in it.

"Somebody's been eating *my* porridge!" Mother Bear cried when she saw her bowl.

"Somebody's been eating my porridge and has finished it all up!" wailed Baby Bear and burst into tears.

Then Father Bear said, "Somebody's been sitting in my chair!"

And Mother Bear said, "Somebody's been sitting in *my* chair *too*!"

And Baby Bear squeaked, "Somebody's been sitting in my chair and has broken it all to *pieces*!"

Then the three bears began to look around for what else they could find.

"Somebody's been sleeping in my bed!" Father Bear growled.

"Somebody's been sleeping in *my* bed *too*!" Mother Bear said.

"Somebody's been sleeping in my bed and here she is *right now*!" cried Baby Bear.

At that, Goldilocks woke up and opened her eyes. When she saw the three bears looking down at her she got such a fright that she jumped off the bed and ran out of the house as fast as she could go. She ran all the way home, and never went into the woods alone again.

# Ali Baba
# & the Forty Thieves

ONCE there lived in a Persian city two brothers named Kassim and Ali Baba. Kassim, who was the elder, married a rich girl, and with her money he bought a big house with plenty of slaves and horses. Ali Baba, however, married a girl as poor as himself; all they owned were three donkeys and three sacks. He used these to pick up firewood which he would sell in the city streets.

One day, as Ali Baba was out collecting wood to fill his sacks, he saw a big cloud of dust on the horizon. As he watched he realized that it was coming towards him, and the earth began to shake under his feet. "The sand out there is being shaken up by a horde of galloping horses," Ali Baba said to himself. "Whoever is on them is in a hurry and won't want me standing in the way." So he climbed up into the nearest tree and hid himself.

Soon a band of robbers came riding up at high speed. Under Ali Baba's tree they drew rein and then dismounted and tethered their

horses. First they fed the horses. Then they unloaded their booty from the horses' backs, piling sacks and sacks of gold and silver in a heap in front of a nearby rock. Then the captain of the band cried out, "Open, Sesamé!" and immediately the stone slid to one side, revealing a cave. The thieves went into the cave one by one, carrying their sacks with them. Ali Baba counted forty of them going in, and forty coming out again. Then their captain said, "Shut, Sesamé" and the rock slid back to its former position. The thieves galloped away, leaving behind them only a cloud of dust.

Ali Baba climbed down the tree as fast as he could, to see for himself what was inside the cave. "Open, Sesamé" he repeated, and waited. The rock slid back, and he stepped into the cave.

He was amazed to see that it was a well-lit vault dug out of the rock and filled to the ceiling with treasure. There were leather bags full of money, rolls of rich brocade and valuable carpets, and chests full of rubies, pearls, and emeralds. Ali Baba heard the door slide closed behind him, but he was not afraid because he knew the password to get out. He carried a few sacks of gold coins to the entrance and said, "Open, Sesamé!" The rock opened as before, and he loaded the sacks onto his donkeys and went back to the city.

When his wife saw the gold she at first thought that he had stolen it, and began scolding him, but when he told her his story she was pleased beyond measure. She began counting the coins one by one, but there were so many that she lost count. So she went to her sister-in-law to borrow her scales to weigh the sacks instead.

"What do you want them for?" asked Kassim's wife suspiciously.

"I can't tell you that!" her sister-in-law replied. Then Kassim and his wife secretly put some wax onto the bottom of the scales, so that whatever was put in the pan would stick.

Having measured the gold, Ali Baba's wife returned the scales without noticing that a piece of gold had stuck to the wax. But when Kassim and his wife saw the coin, they were filled with jealousy.

"Where did you get all that money?" Kassim demanded.

Ali Baba, who was an honest man and a good-natured one too, told his brother everything, even the password into the cave. No sooner had Kassim learned this than he was filled with greed to possess the treasure himself. He saddled ten mules, piled sacks on

their backs, and set off as fast as he could to the place where the cave was hidden. "Open, Sesamé!" he cried, and the walls of the rock slid apart before his eyes. He entered, and the walls closed behind him again.

Kassim was overcome with the sight of so much treasure. He went from one pile to the next, trying to decide which to take first. At last he filled all his sacks and returned to the entrance. But in his greed for the treasure, he had forgotten the password. All

he could remember was that it was the name of some kind of seed.

"Open, barley!" he cried, but the doors remained shut. He tried various other grains, but none would work for him. At length he heard the noise of the robbers dismounting outside the cave, and tried to hide in one of the chests. But they had already discovered his mule and it did not take them long to find him too. The thieves killed Kassim and cut his body into four pieces, which they

placed near the door to frighten away anyone else who might find his way in. Then they rode off again to find some more caravans that they could rob.

When Kassim had not returned by nightfall his wife became anxious and begged Ali Baba to find him. Ali Baba guessed where he was, and set out at once for the cave. He saw blood on the rock, and soon found his brother's body inside the cave. In sorrow he wrapped the four pieces together in a sack,

filled two more sacks with gold, and carried all three back to his sister-in-law.

Kassim's widow wept when she saw her husband's body but she was comforted by her slave Morgiana, a beautiful and intelligent girl. Because they were still afraid of the robbers' revenge, they did not want word to get round that Kassim had been murdered. The slave girl hit upon the plan of getting the most skilled cobbler in the city to come secretly and sew Kassim's body together again so that the corpse could receive a public funeral befitting a man of such enormous wealth.

That night Morgiana went to the cobbler's house. "Come with me," she said to him, "and bring your tools with you." She bandaged his eyes so that he could not see where he was going, and led him to her house. There she commanded him to stitch the body together again, which he did so skilfully that no one would have imagined that Kassim had not died in his sleep. Then she blindfolded the cobbler again and led him back to his shop. Next day Kassim's body was carried in state through the streets, followed by crowds of mourners, and buried in a grave outside the city walls.

"I will move into my brother's house and take over his estate," Ali Baba told Kassim's weeping widow, "if you will become my second wife." She dried her eyes and agreed, for it was common practice in those days for families to keep together in this way.

Meanwhile the forty thieves returned to the cave in the forest, and saw to their fury that another man had found out the secret of the cave. Without delay they dispatched one of the band into the city, to find out who it was. The first man the thief spoke to was Mustapha, the cobbler.

"Has anything extraordinary happened in this city recently?" the thief asked him, and Mustapha replied, "I can't speak for anyone else, but the other night I had to sew a dead man together again, whose body had been cut into four pieces." The thief begged Mustapha to lead him to the house where this had happened, and for the price of a gold coin and a few hides of leather the cobbler agreed to be blindfolded again and successfully led the thief to Kassim's house. The thief marked the door of the house with a white chalk cross, and returned to tell his comrades that he had found out who had stolen their treasure.

Soon afterwards the slave girl Morgiana returned from the market and noticed the strange sign on her master's door. She did not know what it meant, but decided that it would be safest if every door in the street were marked in the same way. So she chalked crosses on all the houses around.

When the thieves came to the street and saw so many white crosses they realized that they had been tricked, and in their fury they stabbed their companion to death. Another thief was sent to find Kassim's house, and again he was led to it by Mustapha in the night. This time he chalked a red circle on the door, and returned to fetch the rest of the band. In the morning, however, Morgiana was up early to fetch the milk, and she noticed the sign on the door. Again she marked all the other houses in the street in the same way, so that the robbers did not know which was the right one, and in their anger they cut off the head of the thief who had led them there.

Then the leader of the band of robbers himself visited Mustapha and was led by him to Kassim's house. Instead of marking the door, however, he made a different plan. He disguised himself as a travelling merchant, selling oil in large jars, and knocked on Ali Baba's door at sunset. Ali Baba did not recognize the robber chief, dressed as he was in a long cloak and leading nineteen mules, each with two large oil jars strapped to its sides. He could not guess that only one of these jars was filled with oil, nor that thirty-seven robbers were hidden in the other jars, each one ready to kill him when their leader gave the word.

"It is late, and I have come far," the robber chief said. "Will you give me shelter for the night and allow me to store my oil jars in your yard?" And Ali Baba, following the custom of Persia, welcomed the traveller to his house, and invited him to eat at his table that night.

As Morgiana began cooking their meal in the kitchen, her oil lamp suddenly ran dry. So she took the empty lamp into the yard to fill it with oil from one of the jars. When she approached the first jar, the robber concealed inside it mistook her for his chief and called out, "Is it time?" Morgiana was startled by the voice but she was a very quick-witted girl. "Not yet!" she replied in as deep a voice as she could. She went to every jar in turn and gave the same answer. Then she filled her biggest kettle with oil from the last jar, and set it on her stove to heat. When the oil was boiling, she carried it back to the yard and tipped some into each jar, scalding the thieves inside to death.

Her master meanwhile was eating and drinking with his guest, and Morgiana continued to wait on them as if nothing had happened. When the meal was over, Ali Baba called to Morgiana to dance for them. She came in wearing a veil and carrying a drum and a jewelled dagger. So well did she dance to the beat of her drum that the robber chief was hypnotized by her sinuous movements. Closer and closer she circled around him—then, suddenly, she stabbed him through the heart.

"What have you done?" cried Ali Baba, rising in horror. Morgiana showed him the hidden knife with which the robber chief was intending to murder his host, and when she led Ali Baba into the yard where the oil jars stood with dead thieves inside them, her master realized how well she had served him and his family.

In gratitude he gave Morgiana her freedom, and soon afterwards his son asked her to become his wife. As a wedding present, Ali Baba told the young couple the password to the cave, so they and their children were able to live in great comfort and happiness for the rest of their days..

# Puss in Boots

THERE was once a poor miller whose only possessions were his mill, a donkey, and a cat. When he died his three sons shared them out as follows: the eldest son took the mill, the middle son the donkey, and the youngest son the cat. The youngest boy was quite dejected at the way their father's property had been divided and felt that he had received a very poor share.

"My brothers can go into partnership and use the donkey to help work the mill, but what use is a cat?" he said to himself. "I could make it into a pie and sell its skin for a muff, but I don't want to kill it."

The cat happened to have overheard his words and spoke up at once. "Don't be

sad, my good master," he said, "just give me a sack and have a pair of boots made up for me, and you will soon see that you had a better bargain than either of your brothers."

The boy was so surprised to hear the cat talk that he was quite ready to believe him. So he went to the best shoemaker in the village and ordered a pair of boots in the softest leather. The cat was so pleased with them that he wore them all the time—which is how he got his name Puss in Boots.

Then the boy gave him the sack he had asked for and Puss in Boots slung it over his shoulder and made for the woods to hunt rabbits. He put some bran and some lettuce into the sack and stretched himself out beside it, pretending to be dead.

He had barely closed his eyes when things began to happen exactly as he had planned. A plump young rabbit hopped out of the bushes, sniffed all round the sack, and then crawled inside it. In a flash the cat drew the string tightly round the top, caught the rabbit, and killed it.

Feeling very pleased that his trick had succeeded so quickly, Puss slung the sack over his shoulder again and set out for the king's palace. Once there, he demanded to see the king without delay, and the flunkeys escorted him to the throne room.

"Sire," he said, bowing, low to the king, I have brought you a young rabbit which my noble lord, the Marquis of Carabas"— for that was the title he had just invented for the miller's son—"has commanded me to present to your majesty."

"Thank your master," the king said graciously, "and tell him I am very pleased with his present."

Another time the cat hid himself in the wheatfields and held his sack wide open. When a couple of partridges fluttered into it, he pulled the string tight and caught them fast. These too he presented to the king, who rewarded Puss suitably.

One day he overheard the courtiers saying that the king was planning to go for a drive along the river with his daughter, who was the most beautiful princess in the world. The cat ran back to his master and said, "If you do as I say, your fortune is made. All you have to do is to go bathing in the river at the exact time and in the exact spot that I tell you. Leave the rest to me."

The young man was very puzzled at this, but he decided to follow the cat's instructions because it was a hot sunny day and he liked swimming in the river anyway. While he was splashing about the king came by in his carriage. At once the cat began to

cry out, "Help! Help! The Marquis of Carabas is drowning! Help! Help!"

As soon as the king heard this name he ordered the carriage to be stopped and commanded his flunkeys to run immediately to rescue the Marquis of Carabas. While they were dragging the boy out of the river, Puss in Boots came up to the carriage and told the king that while his master was bathing, some thieves had come and taken all his clothes away. In fact, the cunning cat had hidden them under a rock.

The king immediately sent an officer off to the palace to fetch one of his best suits for the Marquis of Carabas. Once he was dressed in these new clothes the miller's son was transformed into such a handsome, noble-looking young man that the princess instantly fell in love with him. She persuaded her father to invite him into the royal carriage to accompany them on their drive.

Puss in Boots, who had watched all this with the greatest satisfaction, hurried off ahead of the royal party. Soon he came across some peasants mowing a meadow and said to them, "The king will be driving past soon. When he stops and asks you who owns this meadow that you are mowing, you had better say it belongs to my lord the Marquis of Carabas—for if you don't, you will be chopped into little pieces."

Sure enough, the king ordered his carriage to stop, and asked the mowers to whom the meadows belonged.

"To my lord the Marquis of Carabas," the mowers answered with one voice, for the cat had almost scared them silly.

The king turned to the young man and congratulated him on his fine fertile lands.

Meanwhile the cat ran on ahead once again, and soon came across some reapers reaping a field. Again he told them to say the fields around belonged to the Marquis of Carabas, and again he threatened them with the chopper if they did not. When the king came by a moment later and asked the men who owned the land, they chorused obediently, "To my lord the Marquis of Carabas," and the king once again complimented the young man by his side.

Puss kept running ahead of the royal carriage, and as the king drove on through the countryside he kept hearing the same story.

Finally Puss in Boots came to a stately castle which was owned by an ogre. In fact, it was he who owned all the lands that the king had been riding through. The cat asked to speak to him, saying that his fame had spread far and wide.

The ogre was very flattered at this and invited Puss in Boots to sit down.

"I have heard much about your great skills," the cat went on, "and have been told that you are able to turn yourself into whatever you like. I have heard, for instance, that you can turn yourself into a lion or an elephant or some such wild animal."

"Indeed I can," said the ogre proudly, "and to prove it, I shall show you now." With these words he transformed himself into a lion and let out a great roar which shook the castle walls. Puss in Boots was so frightened that he leaped up onto the roof, which was a dangerous thing to do in his boots. Eventually, when the ogre had resumed his natural form, Puss jumped down again.

"You really scared me," he told the ogre, "but I have also heard it said that you can take on the shape of a tiny creature such as, say, a mouse or a rat. I think *that* would be quite impossible."

"Impossible? Nothing is impossible for me!" exclaimed the ogre, and with that he changed himself into a fieldmouse and began scampering around the floor. With one pounce the cat caught him and ate him up.

Meanwhile the king had seen the castle in the distance and decided to pay a call on its owner. As the carriage rattled over the drawbridge Puss hurried towards it.

"Welcome to the castle of the Marquis of Carabas!" he called, and the king was delighted to hear that his friend lived in such a splendid place.

The young man invited the king and princess into the great hall, where a feast had already been prepared by the ogre for his friends, who were now too scared to come in. When they had finished eating and drinking everything on the tables, the king proposed to the marquis that since he and the princess had obviously fallen in love, they ought to get married. This they promptly did, and lived happily ever after. As for Puss in Boots, he became a great lord and never chased mice again, except for fun.

# Jack & the Beanstalk

Once upon a time there was a poor woman who lived in a humble cottage in the countryside with her only son, whose name was Jack.

They owned a cow that gave more milk than any other cow in the neighbourhood, and they made butter and cheese with the extra milk and sold it at the market nearby. But one day the cow went dry and there was no milk to make butter and cheese. There was not even milk for them to drink. They ate less every day, but before long they had almost nothing left to eat and no money to buy food. Jack was still too young to work and his mother had fallen ill.

Jack's mother called him to her bedside. "I am too weak to go out myself," she told him, "so you must take the cow to market and sell her there for as much money as you can."

Jack liked going to market, but he was sad that they would have to sell the cow. He set out, walking slowly, and had gone about half the way when an old man stopped him.

"Do you want to sell that cow?" he asked Jack. "I'll buy her from you here and now in exchange for these magic beans."

The beans, which were all different colours, were very beautiful, and the old man *had* said they were magic. So Jack gave him the cow and ran home with the beans.

"Look what I've got, mother!" he cried as he hurried into her room. But his mother was furious when she saw that he had come home without any money for the cow. "What!" she cried. "You've sold our good cow for these worthless beans?" And she threw them out of the window.

That evening Jack and his mother ate their last crust of bread and went to bed very sadly, for they knew that there was nothing left for breakfast. Jack woke up early next morning, still hungry. He was so hungry, in fact, that he jumped out of bed and went into the garden to look for something to eat.

To his amazement he saw that the magic beans had grown into a huge plant that stretched right up over the roof and disappeared into the sky. The stems of the plant were so thickly twisted that he could climb up them as if they were the rungs of a ladder. He began to pull himself up higher . . . and higher . . . and higher.

At last he reached the top of the beanstalk. In front of him was a white road, which led to a great castle, far in the distance. There was no one to be seen, so he started to walk along the road. Maybe someone at the castle would give him something to eat. In any

case, it would certainly be an adventure.

He was hot and tired and hungrier than ever by the time he reached the castle. Its great gate was shut, but Jack knocked on it loudly. After a while it was opened by a huge, ugly old woman, who had only one eye, in the middle of her forehead.

"Ah!" she cried. "I need a boy just like you to clean out the fires for me every day! Come in quickly and hide, or my husband will see you and eat you up!"

Frightened, Jack hurried inside at once and told the giantess he would become her servant in exchange for something to eat. She gave him a piece of bread and a glass of buttermilk. But while he was drinking it the castle walls began to shake with a heavy tread and Jack could hear the giant coming closer.

"Quick, hide behind the cupboard," whispered the giantess, and Jack slipped out of sight as the giant stamped into the room shouting:

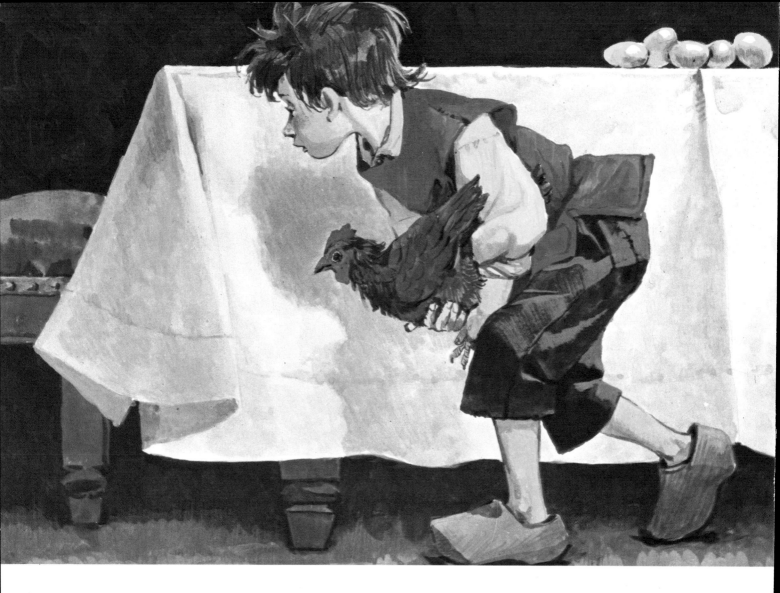

*"Fee, fi, fo, fum,*
 *I smell the blood of an Englishman;*
 *Be he alive or be he dead*
 *I'll grind his bones to make my bread."*

"Nonsense!" said his wife. "It's only a nice young elephant that I've cooked for your breakfast. Sit down and eat it while it's hot."

So the giant sat down, ate his breakfast, and forgot all about the Englishman who stood watching him from behind the cupboard. When he had finished he called out:

"Wife, bring me my magic hen. I want to see some new golden eggs."

Jack could hardly believe his eyes when he saw what happened next. The giantess brought in a little brown hen and put it on the table in front of her husband.

"Lay!" the giant commanded, and plop! plop! plop! she immediately laid one, two, three golden eggs.

The giant scooped the eggs into his pocket. Then he settled back in his chair and soon was snoring so loudly that the castle walls shook with the noise.

Jack crept out from behind the cupboard, snatched up the magic hen, and ran out of the castle as fast as his legs would carry him. With the hen tucked under his arm, he climbed quickly down the beanstalk and hurried into the cottage and up to his mother's room. She was so happy to see him again that she cried for joy, and then she cried some more, because now they would have as many golden eggs as they wanted and need never be poor again.

But Jack soon began to long for another adventure and it was not long before he set out once more to climb the beanstalk higher . . . and higher . . . and higher. He walked up to the giant's castle again and knocked at the gate as before, but this time he had disguised himself so that the old giantess would not recognize him and had dyed his hair orange. He was lucky. The old woman could not see very well with her one eye and she did not know him again.

"Come in," she said, opening the door. "You can wash our clothes and mend our socks. But mind my husband doesn't see you or he will eat you up."

No sooner had Jack entered the castle than the walls began to shake with the giant's heavy footsteps.

"Hurry, hide behind the milk churn," hissed the giantess, and Jack obeyed. The giant's voice filled the room like the roar of the sea:

"Fee, fi, fo, fum,
 I smell the blood of an Englishman;
 Be he alive or be he dead
 I'll grind his bones to make my bread."

"You've got a cold in your nose and you can't smell anything!" scolded his wife. "And if you can, it's only the bull I've roasted for your supper. Eat it up quickly before it gets cold."

So the giant sat down and his wife served the bull on an enormous wooden platter. The two of them ate and ate until there was nothing left on the platter but the bones. Then Jack, who was still crouching behind the milk churn, heard the giant say to his wife, "Woman, bring me my money bags."

She brought him bag after bag of gold pieces and he scattered them on the table and counted the pieces and then put them back in the sacks, one by one. By the time he had closed up the last bag he was yawning, and almost as soon as he lay back in his chair he was fast asleep.

Jack tiptoed across the room, seized the money bags, and ran out of the castle with them, down the beanstalk and back to his mother. She was so glad to see him return safely that she didn't care about the gold in the sacks at all, and scolded him only for taking such risks.

Although there was now more than money enough, Jack's adventurous spirit still sent him climbing up the beanstalk again and again. Each time he dyed his hair

and fooled the giantess anew, each time he hid at sound of the giant's familiar *"Fee, fi, fo, fum,"* and waited to see what he ordered his wife to bring him once he had polished off the sheep, ox or rhinoceros she had roasted for his breakfast or supper. Then, when the giant had done his gloating and fallen into his snoring slumber, Jack would snatch up his latest prize and scramble down the beanstalk again. And if the giant and his wife never suspected that they were being depleted bit by bit of all their treasure, it was because each thought the other had stored it back where it belonged.

Jack's last haul had been a sackful of priceless emeralds and pearls, but the time came when he hankered for one more adventure for its own sake. So one morning he set out again up the beanstalk, higher . . . and higher . . . and higher, until he reached the top. This time he had dyed his hair black, and yet again the giantess did not recognize him.

"Ha! You're just the boy to help me clean out the chicken run and chase the mice away. Hurry inside, for if my husband sees you he will surely eat you up!"

Jack just had time to dart behind the woodpile as the giant came down from his turret, shouting:

*"Fee, fi, fo, fum,*
*I smell the blood of an Englishman;*
*Be he alive or be he dead*
*I'll grind his bones to make my bread."*

"You stupid old giant!" his wife shouted back. "It's only a fat sow which I've grilled for you on the spit. Sit down and eat it up quickly, before it gets cold."

The giant was very pleased for, after Englishmen, grilled pork was his favourite dish. By the end of the meal he felt so cheerful that he called to his wife: "Woman, bring me my magic harp!" and the giantess brought in a beautiful harp, inlaid with rubies and diamonds, which he had stolen from the fairies many years before.

"Play!" he said, and the harp played a soft, sad tune about the green hills and the sea.

"Play something merrier than that!" said the giant. So the harp played a happy tune, which children used to dance to.

"Play me a lullaby now," the giant said, yawning. The harp played a sweet lullaby and soon the giant was fast asleep.

Then Jack crept out from behind the woodpile and picked up the harp, intending to run away with it. But as he seized it, it began to shriek, "Master! Master!" and its strings jangled together and filled the castle with noise. The giant woke up to see Jack running out of the door with the harp.

He leaped up with a roar and lumbered after him, along the road that led to the beanstalk. The earth shook with his heavy tread and Jack could tell he was getting closer all the time. He was very frightened, but he clutched the harp closer and ran on as fast as he could.

At last he reached the beanstalk and began climbing down it as fast as he could with the harp under his arm. He could hear the giant's shouts and feel the beanstalk swaying and shaking under his weight.

Jack's mother was out in the yard and he shouted to her from halfway down the beanstalk, "Quick, mother, bring me an axe!" She ran to the woodshed and came back with the biggest axe she could find.

Jack leaped to the ground, thrust the harp into her arms, and began hacking away at the beanstalk with all his might. "Stand clear, mother!" he shouted. The stalk began to crack and sway from side to side as the giant climbed nearer. Then Jack slashed through the last stem and sprang aside, just in time, as the beanstalk came crashing down, bringing with it the giant, who hit the ground with such a thud that he was killed at once.

Jack had had enough adventures to last him the rest of his life and he and his mother lived happily for many years.

# The Wizard of Oz: Dorothy Kills the Witch

ONCE there was a little girl named Dorothy who lived on a farm in Kansas. One day the sky grew dark and a big wind began to blow across the flat prairies that stretched all around the farm. Dorothy ran into her house to take shelter but the tornado came closer and closer until—suddenly—it lifted Dorothy's house high up into the sky, with Dorothy and her little dog Toto still inside. The house came to rest at last in a magic country, as Dorothy realized the moment she opened the door and walked outside.

The first person she saw was an old lady. She looked just like any other old lady except that she was smaller and wore a high, pointed hat on her head with gold bells hanging from it, and a white gown. She was followed by three small men, all dressed in blue. They too wore high, pointed hats with bells hanging from them, and big boots that reached right over their knees.

"Who are you?" asked Dorothy.

"I am the Witch of the North, and I have come to thank you for killing the Wicked Witch of the East."

Dorothy looked surprised. "I've never killed anybody!" she replied.

"Well, your house did, when it landed here. It fell right on top of her and killed her—you can still see her silver shoes sticking out from under the wall there. Take them; they are yours now."

Dorothy looked down at her own shabby shoes. "Well, it's a long walk back to Kansas from here; I might as well get some good shoes for the journey," she said. "Can you tell me the way home, please?"

"Oh, no, my dear," the old lady replied. "Only the Great Wizard of Oz knows that. You will have to ask him."

"Where does he live?" asked Dorothy.

"A *long* way away, in the Emerald City. The road there is very dangerous."

"Will you come with me?" asked Dorothy.

"No, I can't do that, but I will give you my kiss, and no one will dare to hurt you if you've been kissed by the Witch of the North." She kissed Dorothy softly on the forehead. Where she had kissed her a round, shining mark appeared.

"Thank you," said Dorothy, but before the words were out of her mouth the witch and the three little men had disappeared.

Dorothy put on the silver shoes, tucked Toto under her arm, and set off to find the Wizard of Oz. The road was long, and many

things happened to her on the way there.

First she made friends with a Scarecrow and took him with her on her search. The Scarecrow was going to the Emerald City to ask the Wizard for some brains. The farmer who had made him had stuffed his head with straw, and nobody can think with a head made of straw.

Then she and the Scarecrow came across a Woodman who was made entirely of tin. He begged them to let him join their party, for he wanted the Wizard to give him a heart. A wicked witch had put a spell on his axe one day, and it had cut his body so badly that a smith had had to replace every part of it with tin. The only thing that the smith had not been able to replace had been his heart, and now he wanted more than anything in the world to get a new heart, so that he could feel sorrow and happiness as other people do.

Finally, as they were walking through a dark forest, they met a Lion who had a very fierce roar but who was in fact afraid of everything. Being so cowardly made him very unhappy, for he knew that as king of the beasts he ought to be braver than anyone else.

"Do you think Oz could give me courage?" the Cowardly Lion asked Dorothy.

"Just as easily as he could give me brains," said the Scarecrow.

"Or give me a heart," said the Tin Woodman.

"Or send me back to Kansas," said Dorothy.

"Then, if you don't mind, I'll go with you," said the Lion.

"You're very welcome," answered Dorothy, "for you will help keep away the other wild beasts on our journey."

So off they set, and after a great many adventures they arrived at the gates of the Emerald City.

There they asked to see the Wizard, and one by one they were admitted to his throne room to present their requests. But to each one he gave the same answer, "Your wish will not be granted until you have rid the country of the Wicked Witch of the West." To Dorothy he said, "When you can tell me that the Wicked Witch is dead, I will send you back to Kansas—but not before."

The little girl began to cry, for she thought she couldn't possibly kill the Witch and feared that this meant she would *never* get back to Kansas.

"What shall we do now?" she asked her friends sadly.

"We must go to the land of the West," said the Lion. "We must find this Witch and destroy her."

So they set off towards the Wicked Witch's castle.

It wasn't long before the Witch found out about Dorothy and her party. She was angry with them for coming without

asking her permission first and decided to punish them terribly. She took a tin whistle and blew on it three times.

The whistle was immediately answered by a great howl that seemed to come from all directions at once as a pack of great wolves bounded towards her.

"Go to these strangers," cried the Witch, "and tear them to pieces!"

"Very well," replied the wolves, and off they loped towards the little group.

Luckily the Tin Woodman heard the wolves coming from a long way off. "Let me deal with them," he said. "Get behind me; I'm going to kill them."

He took his axe in both hands and waited for the first wolf. When it was just an arm's length away, he swung the axe into the air and chopped the wolf's head off, and the beast fell dead to the ground. There were

forty wolves in all, and as each one jumped at the Woodman, he knocked it flying. When they all lay dead on the ground, he wiped his axe and put it away.

When the Wicked Witch saw what had happened, she was very angry indeed. She blew another three blasts on her whistle. Immediately a flock of fierce crows flew down and settled at her feet.

"Peck out the strangers' eyes and tear them to pieces!" she commanded them.

The crows flew up and shot off towards Dorothy like so many arrows towards their prey.

The Scarecrow cried, "Let me fight them! Lie down beside me and I will protect you!"

He stretched up his arms and caught each bird as it flew down and broke its neck.

When the Wicked Witch saw all her crows lying dead on the ground, she grew even angrier than before. She blew three more times on her whistle. And at once she was surrounded by a swarm of black bees.

"Go to the strangers and sting them to death!" she cried, and the bees blew off towards Dorothy and her friends like so many bullets shot from a gun.

"Take out my straw stuffing and scatter it over yourselves!" the Scarecrow cried to Dorothy, Toto and the Lion, when he saw the swarm coming. "Then the bees won't be able to sting you!" They did as he said, and when the bees came down they found no one but the Tin Woodman to sting. They flew at him and broke their stings against his tin body and fell dead to the ground.

Then Dorothy and the Lion and Toto got up and stuffed the straw into the Scarecrow again, and they continued their journey.

The Wicked Witch turned purple with anger when she saw that her precious bees too had been killed by the strangers. She called her slaves, the Winkies, and told them to take their sharpest spears and kill the five of them at once.

So the slaves set off down the road, but they were frightened because they knew what had happened to the wolves and the crows and the bees.

When the Lion saw the Winkies coming, he gave a great roar and sprang towards them. "Help!" they cried, and scuttled off back to the castle as fast as they could run.

Then the Wicked Witch sat down and began to think hard. She could not understand how she had failed to destroy the little group, and she was more determined than ever to kill them.

She had in her safe a golden cap with a circle of diamonds and rubies curling around it. This was a magic cap, for whoever owned it could call on the winged monkeys and make them carry out any order they were given. But no one could call on the monkeys more than three times. Twice already the Wicked Witch had made them do her bidding. She could use the cap to call the monkeys only once more, and she did not want to do this until all her other magic had been used up. But she had tried everything she could against the strangers: her wolves and her crows and her bees were dead, and her slaves had been scared away. There was only the golden cap left.

The Witch took it out of her safe and put it on her head. Slowly she intoned in a chant.

*"Ep-pe, pep-pe, kak-ke!"*

Suddenly the sky went black, and a low

rumbling like the sea breaking over rocks could be heard. The air was filled with winged monkeys as they flocked into the castle. The biggest one among them flew up to her and said:

"For the third and last time we come at your call, Wicked Witch of the West. What do you want?"

"Go to the strangers and destroy them all except the Lion. Bring him to me. I want to harness him like a pony and make him drive me around."

"We go at your command," said the leader, as they flew off towards Dorothy and her friends. They swooped down and picked up the Tin Woodman and carried him through the air to a rocky place. There they dropped him so that he crashed down onto the rocks and was so battered and dented that he could not move.

Then they picked up the Scarecrow and began tearing the stuffing out of his body. When they had scattered the straw, they tied up his clothes and threw them into a tree.

They threw coils of strong rope around the Lion and tied him up like a parcel. Then they lifted him up and flew away with him to the Witch's castle.

Dorothy was very frightened when she saw what the monkeys were doing to her friends. She stood with Toto in her arms watching them, knowing that it would be her turn next. The leader of the monkeys flew up to her and stretched out his long, hairy arms to snatch her away. Then he stopped suddenly. His face was quite close to hers, and he was looking at the round, shining mark that the kiss from the Good Witch of the North had left on Dorothy's smooth young forehead.

"Don't hurt her!" he cried. "She is protected by the power of good! It's much more powerful than the power of evil is!"

So they lifted Dorothy up gently and carried her through the air to the castle. Dorothy squeezed Toto tightly under her arm, and together they were set down in front of the Witch.

"We have obeyed you as far as we could," the monkey leader told her. "We dare not harm either the little girl or her dog. Now your power over us is ended, and you will never see us again." With that the monkeys flew off and disappeared into thin air.

The Wicked Witch was angry when she saw the shining circle that the Good Witch's kiss had left on Dorothy, for she knew now that she could not hurt her in any way. Then she noticed that

Dorothy was wearing magic shoes and that she did not seem to know they were magic. A cunning gleam came into the Witch's eye.

"Come here at once!" she shouted at Dorothy. "You must do exactly as I tell you. If you don't, I shall kill you as I have killed the Woodman and the Scarecrow!" She ordered Dorothy to set to work to clean up the whole castle and to stoke the fire in the kitchen. Then she went out into the yard to

see the Lion who had been shut up there.

"How grand I shall look," she thought, "when I'm driven through the streets by a lion." She opened the door cautiously. The Lion leapt up. "Arr-rr!" he roared, and the Witch's teeth rattled together in fear.

She jumped back to a safer distance and shouted at him, "If you don't do as I say, I shall starve you to death!" "Arr-rr!" the Lion replied and shook his mane.

When the Witch went to bed that night, Dorothy crept into the yard and brought him some food. She came to him every night and talked to him, trying to work out a means of escape for them both. But every gate and bridge around the castle was guarded by the Witch's slaves.

"I *must* get hold of Dorothy's magic shoes!" the Witch said to herself. "When I have them, I'll be so powerful that I'll have no more worries on earth." But Dorothy never took off her shoes except at night and when she went to have a bath. The Witch was too afraid of the dark to steal them in the night, and she was even more afraid of water. In fact she always made quite sure that she kept right away from even the tiniest splash and carried an umbrella with her wherever she went.

Eventually the Witch tried to steal the shoes away by a trick. She put an iron bar in the middle of the kitchen and cast a spell on it to make it invisible. Dorothy did not see it and so she fell right over it. One of her shoes flew off and the Witch snatched it up at once.

"Ha-ha! It's mine now and you can't work the spell any more, even if you knew how to!" she said.

"I've got no idea what you're talking about," said Dorothy crossly. "Give me back my shoe at once!"

"I will not," hissed the Witch. "It's my shoe now!"

"You are wicked!" cried Dorothy. "That shoe belongs to me!"

"I shall keep it just the same, and some day I'll get the other one from you too!"

This made Dorothy so angry that she picked up the bucket of water she had just pumped up and threw it over the Witch, soaking her from head to foot.

"Aaah! Iiih!" screamed the Witch. She

began to shake and melt away at the edges. "See what you've done!" she cried. "I'm going to evaporate!"

"I'm sorry," stammered Dorothy, who was really frightened to see the Witch melting away before her eyes. "Was there anything wrong with that water?"

"No, there wasn't. But any sort of water is the death of me. Oh dear, oh dear, here I go!" And with these words the Witch melted right away into a little brown puddle.

Dorothy put her second silver shoe back on again. Then she picked up the Witch's bunch of keys and ran out into the yard to unlock the Lion's cage. "We're free! We're free! The Wicked Witch is dead!" she cried.

How Dorothy and her friends were reunited, how the Wizard of Oz granted them all their wishes, and how the little girl found her way back at last to her home in Kansas is a long story which you must find in another book.

45

# The Princess & the Pea

THERE was once a prince who wanted to get married. Being a prince, of course he had to marry a princess, but he had been brought up by his mother, the queen, to be very particular. She must be a real princess, he insisted; nothing less would do. There were no princesses in his own kingdom, so he travelled all over the world searching for one. But every princess who was introduced to him seemed to have some fault. Either her feet were too big or her nose was too long or her voice was too squeaky. He just couldn't find a real princess anywhere. So he returned to his kingdom very disappointed and thinking he would have to give up the idea of marrying altogether.

One night soon after he got back the rain began to fall in torrents and lightning and thunder shook the sky. Everyone was crouched around their fires listening to the wind when a knock was heard at the palace gate. The old king put on his boots and went to open it.

There, standing in the rain, was a princess. But what a sight she looked! Her golden hair stuck to her graceful neck and the rain was running out of her silk shoes. Yet she said she was a real princess. She said she was on her way home to her own country from a visit to a neighbouring kingdom when she was caught by the rain.

"We'll soon see about that," thought the queen when the princess was brought inside and introduced to everyone. "That's the most unlikely story I've ever heard. No real princess could ever look so bedraggled."

Guarding against being watched, the cunning old queen thereupon took a dried pea from a kitchen jar, went cautiously up to the guest room and put it in the centre of the princess's bed. Next she smuggled twenty mattresses out of the linen closets and laid them one after another on top of the pea. You never saw such an assortment of mattresses!

They were all of the finest quality of

course; in this, as in all else, only the best would have found a place in the fussy queen's household. So out came a mattress of goose feathers stitched into quilted pale pink satin, another of lustrous purple silk enfolding the fleeciest lamb's wool, a third of the purest white muslin encasing a billow of swansdown. There were striped mattresses, sprigged mattresses, brocade, linen and lawn mattresses. And yet to come were mattresses of the supplest cloth of gold interwoven with the royal initials and the royal coat of arms. Finally, the queen topped off all these accumulated layers with twenty feather quilts.

"There!" she murmured at last, huffing and puffing a bit by now after so much unwonted effort. "*Now* we'll see whether she's a real princess or not!"

In the morning the princess came down to breakfast look- ing very tired. "Did you sleep well?" asked the old queen.

"No I didn't," replied the princess. "I don't know what was in the bed. Something as hard as a rock and as big as a cannonball. In fact I think it *was* a cannonball—I'm bruised black and blue all over."

Then everyone smiled with delight, for now they knew that she was a real princess: no one else could have such delicate skin. The prince immediately took her for his wife. As for the pea, it was taken out of the bed and put in the royal museum, where it probably remains to this day.

# Little Red Riding Hood

ONCE upon a time there was a little girl who lived with her mother in a cottage on the edge of a large forest. Her grandmother, who doted on her, had made her for her birthday a red velvet bonnet with a tunic to match to wear over her dresses. The child liked the costume so much that she wore it every day wherever she went, until her real name was altogether forgotten and everyone who knew her called her Little Red Riding Hood instead.

One day when she was playing in the garden her mother called her and told her that she had just baked a cake which she would like Little Red Riding Hood to take with a bottle of wine to her grandmother who had fallen ill and had to stay in bed.

"As your grandmother is all alone in her house in the forest," she said, "she will be glad of your company. And this cake and the wine will do her good. Tell her I shall come myself a little later on when I am less busy." She wrapped the cake in a cloth and laid it carefully beside the bottle of wine in a basket. "Now see to it," she admonished, "that you don't stray off the path. And don't on any account talk to strangers."

Little Red Riding Hood dearly loved her grandmother, so she took the basket and set off eagerly, very proud to be entrusted with such an important errand. She was not often allowed to go so far from her home alone and, heeding what her mother had said, kept close to the path, taking care not to stumble over the sticks and stones as she ran along humming a little tune to herself. She looked very pretty with the ribbons of her red bonnet flying out above her long flaxen hair, and around her waist a blue sash the same colour as the dress that peeped out beneath her beloved red tunic.

She had to slow down when she reached the forest itself, where the trees grew thicker and the path more winding. And it was there that she met the wolf.

She had never heard of a wolf, and certainly never seen one and, having no notion of his evil cunning, was not the least bit frightened of him. It didn't enter her head that anyone would want to harm such a little thing as herself anyway.

"Good morning," said the wolf. "What a pretty red riding hood you're wearing."

The child was so pleased to hear this that she immediately forgot what her mother had said about not talking to strangers. She had always been a friendly little girl.

"Yes, isn't it," she replied. "My granny made it for my birthday. She is ill in bed and I am on my way to visit her."

"And what have you got in your basket, Little Red Riding Hood?" the wolf inquired politely.

"A cake my mother baked and some wine that we hope will make granny feel better." She held out the basket so that the wolf could have a peep inside.

"Where does your grandmother live, Little Red Riding Hood?" asked the wolf.

"She lives in the cottage next to the three oak trees in the middle of the forest."

"What a tasty little creature she does look," the wolf thought to himself, unable to keep his hungry eyes off the child. "How I'd like to eat her up this very minute. But if I'm clever I shall be able to have both her *and* her grandmother for my lunch today."

So he walked along beside Little Red Riding Hood, making amiable conversation about the beautiful morning and what a lucky little girl she was to be visiting her grandmother, while what he was really up to was trying to think of a way of delaying her so that he could reach the grandmother's

house before Little Red Riding Hood did.

Suddenly an idea came to him and he said, "Look at those lovely ripe strawberries over there and all those flowers growing under the trees. Wouldn't it be nice if you picked some to take to your grandmother?"

Little Red Riding Hood needed no persuading. She was usually an obedient little girl, but she at once forgot her other promise to her mother not to leave the path. The sunlight filtering through the trees seemed to beckon to her, and all the berries and the flowers looked so tempting that she simply *had* to pick some. Waving goodbye to the wolf, she disappeared into the forest.

Meanwhile the wolf wasted no time. With a leap and a bound he made straight off for the grandmother's cottage by a short cut and was soon knocking at the door.

"Who is there?" the old lady called out feebly from her bed.

"It's Little Red Riding Hood, granny dear, I've brought you a cake and some wine," said the wolf, trying to imitate the little girl's high-pitched squeaky voice.

"Let yourself in, my dear," replied the grandmother. "I am too weak to get up. Just lift the latch."

The wolf quickly opened the door and took a stealthy look around the room. Then in one great spring he leaped up onto the grandmother's bed and before she could let out so much as a whimper gobbled her up, nightclothes and all, in a few greedy swallows. Feeling somewhat less ravenous, he bounded across to a chest in the corner where he rummaged until he found another of the old lady's neatly folded nightgowns and caps. Slipping these on, he hastily drew the curtains to make the room a shade darker, scrambled back into the bed, and crouched down low between the sheets.

Little Red Riding Hood lost all thought of the time as she darted about picking flowers and berries. The ripe strawberries, red as her bonnet, looked so enticing that she popped almost as many into her mouth as she did into her basket. As for the flowers, there were so many that she scarcely knew which to choose, so she ran from one spot to another, trying to pick as many different colours as possible. It was only when she had gathered as many as her basket and hands could hold that she remembered her errand.

By now she had wandered so deep into the forest that she had to heed her step through the tangled bushes a little more carefully on the way back. And there were still things to distract her. A bushy-tailed squirrel didn't seem to mind such a little girl watching him bury a nut, then smooth the earth over his hiding place with his skilful paws. And what child could have resisted chasing the prettiest orange-speckled yellow butterfly until it had fluttered out of reach, or not stopped to cock an eye and an ear at a woodpecker tapping its sharp bill against the bark of a tree?

Even when she was back once more on the familiar path she still couldn't help dawdling a little, to watch a bird flapping its wings overhead or hopping about underfoot, to sniff at her posy of white, yellow, blue, red and purple wildflowers.

But eventually she reached her grandmother's cottage and knocked at the door.

"Who is there?" called the wolf, trying

hard this time to imitate the old lady's voice.

"It's Little Red Riding Hood, granny dear. I've brought you a cake my mother baked for you and some wine to make you better. And I picked some flowers and berries for you in the forest."

"Lift the latch and come right in, dear," the wolf called back as gently as he could. He had become rather impatient and cross as he waited, thinking that perhaps he had been altogether too wily for his own good and that the little girl was going to cheat him of the juiciest part of his lunch by not coming.

Little Red Riding Hood did as she was told and easily lifted the simple latch. She always enjoyed coming to see her grandmother, but now as she crossed the threshold into the cottage she suddenly felt disquiet without really knowing why. Hesitating a moment, she squinted her eyes around the darkened room, surprised that her grand-

mother should want to keep the curtains closed and shut out the sparkling sunshine which would surely cheer her up if she wasn't feeling well. Setting down her basket and the flowers, she tiptoed gingerly over to the large bed and was just about to give her grandmother a kiss as usual when she drew back a step with an uneasy start.

"Why, granny," she exclaimed wonderingly, "what big ears you have!"

"All the better to hear you with, my dear," came the reply. The old lady's voice sounded rather croaky, but Little Red Riding Hood thought she must have a cold. It was something much stranger about her grandmother that made her peer even more anxiously at the bed.

"Why, granny, what big eyes you have!"

"All the better to see you with, my dear."

The child's own eyes were by now almost as round as a small owl's.

"Why, granny, what enormous big hands you have!"

"All the better to hold you with, my dear."

"And, oh granny! What terribly big teeth you have."

"ALL THE BETTER TO EAT YOU WITH, MY DEAR!"

And with these ominous words the wolf reached out his great claws, grabbed hold of Little Red Riding Hood and gobbled her up in no time at all, licking his thick lips after each tender mouthful. Feeling very bloated indeed after such a sumptuous meal, he then stretched himself out to his full length on the bed, settled his head comfortably back on the pillow and was soon sound asleep, snoring loudly enough to shake the rafters.

A short while afterwards a huntsman, gun swinging from his shoulder, happened to pass that way. Thinking that something must be seriously wrong with the old lady to make her snore so raucously, he rapped on the door in case she should be in need of help. And when there was no answer, he too lifted the latch and let himself into the cottage. A few long strides brought him to the foot of the bed where he was nearly startled out of his wits to discover the wolf lying there in the old lady's stead.

"You old rogue," he muttered to himself, "so I've got you at last! I've been on your trail long enough!" and he whipped the gun off his shoulder and shot the wolf dead.

It was only then that the huntsman noticed not only that the wolf was wearing the old lady's nightclothes, but how fat he looked bulging there under the counterpane.

"So that's where she is!" he guessed out loud, and there being no sign of the old lady anywhere else, he pulled his hunting knife from his satchel and slit open the wolf's stomach from end to end. And out tumbled the old lady and Little Red Riding Hood, both of them still alive, although stiff from being so cramped, and obviously shaken by their frightening experience.

It wasn't long, however, before the two of them recovered. The huntsman sat the old

lady in an armchair and wrapped a blanket around her, but once she had eaten two slices of the cake and drunk a glassful of the wine, she declared she didn't need fussing over any more and was well enough to get dressed. And dress herself she did in her best pink dress, as if she were giving a party.

"And it really *is* like a party," Little Red Riding Hood thought, nibbling at the cake she was sharing with her grandmother and the huntsman. The porch of the cottage bloomed gaily with flowers, none gayer than her own posies arranged in a handsome pink bowl. No one had scolded her and when the huntsman slung the wolf over his shoulder and waved goodbye, she felt she had made a new friend.

But you can be sure that she never left the path or spoke to a stranger again.

# Snow White & the Seven Dwarfs

ONCE upon a time a queen sat sewing by her window. The snow was falling outside, and she watched the flakes settle on her black ebony window sill. As she sewed, she pricked her finger with the needle and a drop of red blood fell onto the snow. She thought to herself:

"I wish I had a daughter with skin as white as this snow, with lips as red as this blood, and with hair as black as this ebony."

By and by her wish came true and she gave birth to a baby girl whom she called Snow White. But the queen died when her baby was born and not long afterwards the king married again. The new queen was very beautiful, but she was an evil woman and could not bear the idea that anyone might be lovelier than she.

A magic mirror hung in her room and each day she would look in it and ask:

*"Mirror, mirror on the wall,*
*Who is the fairest of us all?"*

And the mirror would reply:

*"You, O queen, are fairer than all."*

The years went by and each day Snow White grew more beautiful until one morning, when the queen looked yet again into her mirror and asked:

*"Mirror, mirror on the wall,*
*Who is the fairest of us all?"*

it replied:

*"You are fair, O queen, it's true*
*But Snow White is fairer far than you!"*

The queen was beside herself with hatred and jealousy, and resolved to get rid of her stepdaughter at once. She sent for a huntsman and ordered him to take the girl deep into the forest and kill her—and bring back her heart as proof that she was dead.

The huntsman rode with Snow White into the deepest part of the forest, but when he took out his knife to kill her he was so touched by the girl's beauty and gentleness that he could not plunge its blade through her heart.

"I cannot kill you myself," he said, "but I cannot take you back to the palace, and I fear the wild beasts of the forest will soon eat you up."

He left Snow White in the forest, and on his way back he killed a deer instead and gave its heart to the queen, who believed that it was Snow White's.

Poor Snow White, meanwhile, was wandering in the dark forest, terrified. The wild beasts watched her as she stumbled through the trees, but they did not touch her. At nightfall she came to a clearing in the wood, where there was a little house. She tapped on the shutters, but no one answered. She tapped on the door, and then opened it and went inside.

She found herself in a low room with a wooden table and benches stretching the length of it. On the table were seven bowls, seven spoons, and seven cups. For this was the home of the seven dwarfs, who worked in the mountains digging for gold.

Snow White was so hungry that she sat down and ate a little of the pudding in each bowl and sipped some milk from each cup. Then she went upstairs, where there was a

room just large enough to hold seven small beds. She slipped into one of them and was soon fast asleep.

As the moon came up in the sky the seven dwarfs returned. Each carried his shovel and pickaxe on his back and his bags of gold tied to his waist with a leather strap. As soon as they set their lanterns on the table, they saw someone had been in their house.

"Who has been eating our food?" they cried. Then they climbed upstairs to the bedroom and found Snow White asleep on a bed.

"And who is this beautiful child?" they asked each other in delight and amazement.

Then Snow White awoke and told them her story, and the dwarfs felt so sorry for her that they invited her to stay with them and be their housekeeper. They warned her that she must never open the door to anyone while they were away digging in the mountains, for they feared that the wicked queen would find out she was alive and try to kill her.

So Snow White stayed with the dwarfs, and made their beds and swept their rooms and cooked supper for them. She was very happy with the dwarfs and before long she had forgotten all about her wicked step-mother.

One day, however, the queen again asked her magic mirror:

"Mirror, mirror on the wall,
   Who is the fairest of us all?"

and the mirror replied:

"You are fair, O queen, it's true
   But Snow White is fairer far than you.
   Deep within the forest glade
   She her home with dwarfs has made."

The queen's face turned black with rage at these words. Realizing the huntsman had tricked her, she resolved to kill Snow White with her own hands. She disguised herself as a pedlar woman and made her way to the dwarfs' house in the forest. Snow White was sitting by the window, patching a jacket belonging to one of the dwarfs. The queen called out to her in a rough countrywoman's voice:

*"Buy my buttons, ribbons, lace,*
*Every one will suit your face."*

Delighted at the chance of buying something pretty, Snow White quite forgot the dwarfs' warning. She ran to open the door.

"The laces on your bodice are loose, my dear," said the disguised queen. "Let me tie them up for you!"

And with that she laced Snow White up so swiftly and so tightly that the girl could not breathe and fell to the ground as if she were dead. Laughing, the wicked queen hurried back to her palace, feeling certain she had got rid of Snow White for good.

When the dwarfs came home that night, they found Snow White lying in the doorway. As soon as they lifted her up, they could see what had happened. They cut the laces on her bodice with a knife and at once the air rushed back into Snow White's lungs and she began breathing again. She told them what had happened, and the dwarfs realized that the pedlar woman was the wicked queen in disguise, still determined to kill her.

"Never open the door to *anyone* again," they begged her, and Snow White promised she would not.

That night the queen went to her mirror again.

*"Mirror, mirror on the wall,*
*Who is the fairest of us all?"*

she asked, and the mirror replied:

*"You are fair, O queen, it's true*
*But Snow White is fairer far than you."*

The evil queen's blood ran cold as she heard this, and she could not rest until she had made a new plan to kill Snow White. Again she disguised herself as a pedlar woman, but this time she looked completely different and much younger. When she came to the dwarfs' house she tapped on the door and Snow White came to the window and looked out. Delighted by the combs and jewellery the pedlar woman carried on her tray, she opened the window so that she could see better.

"You have such pretty things," she said, "but I can't come out to buy anything, for I have promised I won't open the door to strangers."

"Take a look at this, my dear," urged the queen, holding up a beautiful comb made of tortoiseshell and gold.

Snow White was so interested in the comb that she forgot all about her promise and came out of the house to look at it more closely.

"Let me comb your hair with it," coaxed the queen, and she started to draw the comb through Snow White's shining black hair. But it had been dipped into a deadly poison and its teeth had only to graze Snow White's scalp for the poison to take effect. She fell to the ground in a dead faint, and the queen went away smiling with hatred.

That day the seam of gold that the dwarfs were mining ended sooner than they had expected and they came home unusually early. There they found Snow White lying as if she were dead with the poisoned comb still in her hair. They snatched it out, and as they did so she opened her eyes and smiled at them. When they heard what had happened, they warned her that the pedlar had been her stepmother and begged her never to open the door to anyone again.

The queen, meanwhile, had returned to the palace in triumph. She went straight to her mirror and asked:

*"Mirror, mirror on the wall,*
*Who is the fairest of us all?"*

But the mirror, which could only speak the truth, replied:

*"Your poison was in vain, O queen,*
*Snow White's beauty reigns supreme."*

At this the enraged queen rushed to her cellar in the castle where she kept her secret potions. There she made a poisoned apple. One side was bright red, the other green. The green side could safely be eaten, but one bite of the red side would kill in a second.

Yet again the queen disguised herself. This time she dressed as a countrywoman in ragged clothes with a basket of apples over her arm. On top of the pile she placed the

beautifully coloured poisoned apple.

She arrived at the dwarfs' house just as Snow White was drawing water from the well. But as soon as the girl saw her coming she grew frightened and ran indoors, bolting the door behind her.

Then she heard the voice of the country-woman calling:

*"Apples, fresh and sweet,*
*Apples!"*

and she longed to taste them. If she opened the window and kept the door shut, there could be no danger. So she opened the shutter and leaned out.

"Let me see your apples," she called down.

"Taste this one, my pretty, it's one of the best," replied the queen, holding up the poisoned apple. Then, as the girl hesitated, she went on, "Don't be afraid to eat it. See, I'll cut it in two halves, one for you and one for me."

She began to eat the green half and threw

the red one up to Snow White, who could not resist taking a bite. But she had no sooner put the apple into her mouth than she fell to the ground, dead.

That night the queen polished and stroked the mirror as she asked:

*"Mirror, mirror in my hand,*
*Who is the fairest in the land?"*

and the mirror replied:

*"Queen of beauty, you are she,*
*None can now your rival be!"*

When the dwarfs came home and found Snow White dead beyond reviving, they built a glass coffin which they set among flowers nearby so they could watch over her day and night.

One day a young prince came riding by with huntsmen. Seeing the glass coffin, he dismounted from his horse, curious for a look at the girl inside. She seemed to be in a deep sleep, for her skin was still as white as snow, her lips as red as blood, and her hair as black as ebony. Her beauty en-enchanted him.

"Let me carry the coffin away with me," he begged the dwarfs. "I will give you greater riches than you can ever hope to dig out of these mountains."

"No," the dwarfs replied. "She is worth more to us than all the gold in the world."

But at last, when they saw that the prince had fallen in love with their dear Snow White, they took pity on him and gave him the coffin as a present.

The prince told his huntsmen to carry the glass case carefully to his palace, but as they were lifting it up one of them stumbled over a root, and the jarring made the piece of apple fall from between Snow White's lips. She awoke and sat up, looking about her in

the banquet she asked the mirror:

*"Mirror, mirror on the wall*
*Who is the fairest of us all?"*

and the mirror replied:

*"Fairer than you was rarely seen,*
*But Snow White too is now a queen;*
*Your fairness, then, is nothing worth*
*Now Snow White's radiance fills the*
*earth!"*

When she heard this the queen smashed the mirror in pieces to the ground, and she was so filled with a jealous rage that her heart burst and she fell down dead. But Snow White and her prince lived happily ever after.

amazement. The prince told her everything that had happened, and then asked her to become his wife. And Snow White, who had loved him the moment she set eyes on him, happily agreed.

A great feast was held in honour of their marriage and one of the guests invited was the wicked queen. As she robed herself for

# The Wonderful Tar-Baby

MANY years ago there was a little boy who lived on a cotton plantation in the American South. His best friend was an old black man called Uncle Remus whom he was always begging for another story about Brer Rabbit, and Brer Fox who was always trying to catch him. But the rabbit was too smart and always got away.

"Didn't the fox *never* catch the rabbit, Uncle Remus?" the boy asked one evening.

"He come mighty near it one time, honey. One day Brer Fox got him some tar, an' he mixed it in with some turpentine an' fixed up a contraption that he called a Tar-Baby. An' he set this here Tar-Baby right smack in the big road an' then lay down in the bushes an' watched for to see what would happen.

"Pretty soon Brer Rabbit come prancin' along the road, lippity-clippity, sassy as a jaybird, till he spied the Tar-Baby sittin' there, an' then he fetched up on his hind legs lookin' mighty astonished. The Tar-Baby just sat there, doin' nothin', an' Brer Fox, he kept on layin' low.

" 'Mornin'!' says Brer Rabbit. 'Nice weather this mornin',' says he.

"Tar-Baby ain't sayin' nothin', an' Brer Fox, he lay low.

" 'How is the state of your health at present?' says Brer Rabbit to Tar-Baby. An' when there ain't no answer, 'Is you deaf?' he says, 'because if you is, I can holler louder.'

"Brer Fox wink slow, but Tar-Baby just sat.

" 'You're mighty stuck up, you is,' says Brer Rabbit. 'An' I'm goin' to cure you,' says he. 'I'm goin' to learn you how to talk to respectable people if it's the last thing I do,' he says. 'If you don't take off that old hat an' say howdy-do to me, I'm goin' to bust you wide open,' says Brer Rabbit.

"Brer Fox, he sorta chuckled, but Tar-Baby kept on sayin' nothin', till finally Brer Rabbit draw back his fist and *blip*—he hit Tar-Baby right smack on the side of the head. Right there's where Brer Rabbit made his big mistake. His fist stuck fast in the tar an' he couldn't pull loose. But Tar-Baby, he just sat. An' Brer Fox, he lay low.

" 'If you don't let me loose, I'll knock you again,' says Brer Rabbit, an' with that he fetched Tar-Baby a swipe with the other hand. An' *that* stuck. Tar-Baby she ain't sayin' nothin', an' Brer Fox, he lay low.

" 'Turn me loose,' hollers Brer Rabbit. 'Turn me loose before I kick the natural stuffin' out of you,' he says. But Tar-Baby ain't sayin' nothin'—just keeps on holdin' fast. Then Brer Rabbit he commenced to kick, an' the next thing he know his feet are stuck fast too. Brer Rabbit squall out that if Tar-Baby didn't turn him loose, he'd butt with his head. Brer Rabbit butted, an' then he got his head stuck too.

"Then Brer Fox, he sauntered out of the bushes, lookin' as innocent as a mockin' bird.

" 'Howdy, Brer Rabbit,' says Brer Fox, says he. 'You look sort of stuck up this mornin',' says he, an' then he rolled on the ground and he laughed and laughed till he couldn't laugh no more. 'I reckon you're goin' to have dinner with me this time, Brer Rabbit,' he says. 'I've laid in a heap o' nice vegetables an' things, an' I ain't goin' to take no excuse,' says Brer Fox."

Here Uncle Remus paused and raked a sweet potato out of the ashes on the hearth.

"Did the fox eat the rabbit, Uncle Remus?" asked the little boy.

"Well, now, that's as far as the tale goes," replied the old man. "Maybe he did—an' then again, maybe he didn't."

# How Brer Rabbit Fooled Brer Fox

ONE evening, when the little boy had finished supper and hurried out to sit with his friend, he found the old man in great glee. Uncle Remus was talking and laughing to himself at such a rate that the little boy was afraid that he had company. The truth is, Uncle Remus had heard the child coming and, when the little chap put his head in at the door, was busy talking to himself and humming words that went something like this:

*"Old Molly Har*
 *What you doing thar,*
 *Sitting in the corner*
 *Smoking your cigar?"*

Whatever this meant, it somehow reminded the little boy that the wicked Fox was still chasing the Rabbit, and he immediately said:

"Uncle Remus, did the Rabbit have to go right away from there, when he got loose from the Tar-Baby?"

"Bless you, honey, no he didn't. Who? Him? You don't know nothing at all about Brer Rabbit if that's the way you think he is. What should he go away for? He maybe stayed sorta close till the tar rubbed off his hair some. But it wasn't many days before he was loping up and down the neighbourhood the same as ever—and I don't know if he wasn't even more cheeky than before.

"Seems like the tale about how he got mixed up with the Tar-Baby got round among the neighbours. Leastways, the girls got wind of it, and the next time Brer Rabbit paid them a visit they tackled him about it. The girls giggled, but Brer Rabbit

he just sat there as cool as a cucumber, he did, and let them run on. Like a lamb, he sat there, and then by and by he crossed his legs and leant back and winked his eye slowly. Then he got up and said:

" 'Ladies, Brer Fox was my daddy's

riding horse for thirty years—maybe more, but thirty years that I know about,' said he. Then he paid the ladies his respects, and he tipped his hat, he did. And off he marched, just as stiff and stuck up as a stick.

"Next day Brer Fox came a calling on the ladies and when he began to laugh about Brer Rabbit the gals they got up and told him about what Brer Rabbit said. Well, Brer Fox he grit his teeth and he looked mighty grumpy. But when he got up to go he said, said he:

" 'Ladies, I ain't disputing what you say, but I tell you this: I'll make Brer Rabbit chew up his words and spit 'em out right here where you can see 'em,' said he. And with that, off went Brer Fox.

"As soon as he got to the road, Brer Fox shook the dew off his tail and made a straight shoot for Brer Rabbit's house. Brer Rabbit was expecting him, of course, and when he got there, the door was shut fast. Brer Fox knocked. Nobody answered. Brer Fox knocked again. Nobody answered. Brer Fox kept on knocking—then Brer Rabbit hollered out, but mighty weak:

" 'Is that you, Brer Fox? I want you to run and fetch the doctor. Something I ate

this morning is killing me. Please Brer Fox, run quick, quick,' says Brer Rabbit, says he.

" 'I just come to get you, Brer Rabbit,' says Brer Fox. 'There's going to be a party up at the girls' house and I promised that I'd fetch you.'

"Brer Rabbit said he was too sick to go. Brer Fox said he wasn't—and then they had it up and down, disputing and contending. Brer Rabbit said he couldn't walk. Brer Fox said he'd carry him. Brer Rabbit said, How? and Brer Fox said, In his arms.

Brer Rabbit said he was afraid he'd drop him. Brer Fox promised he wouldn't.

"By and by Brer Rabbit said he'd go if Brer Fox let him ride on his back. Brer Fox said he'd do that. But Brer Rabbit said he couldn't ride without a saddle. Brer Fox said he would get a saddle. Brer Rabbit said he couldn't sit in the saddle unless he had a bridle to hold on to. Brer Fox said he'd get the bridle. But Brer Rabbit said he couldn't ride without blinkers on the bridle because Brer Fox might shy at stumps along the way and fling him off. Brer Fox said he'd get a bridle with blinkers.

"Then Brer Rabbit said he'd go. And Brer Fox said he'd ride Brer Rabbit most of the way up to the girls' house, but then he'd let him get down and walk the rest of the way. Then Brer Rabbit agreed.

"Of course, Brer Rabbit knew all along the sort of trick that Brer Fox was meaning to play on him, and he determined to outdo him. Well, by the time he'd combed his hair and smoothed it down, and twisted and twirled his moustache and spruced himself up, along came Brer Fox with the saddle and bridle strapped on, looking as pert as a circus pony. So Brer Rabbit hopped on him and they ambled off.

"Brer Fox couldn't see behind because of the blinkers he was wearing, but by and by he felt Brer Rabbit raise one of his feet.

" 'Well, what are you doing, Brer Rabbit?' said he.

" 'Shortening the left stirrup, Brer Fox,' said he.

"By and by Brer Rabbit raised up the other foot.

" 'What are you doing now, Brer Rabbit?' said he.

" 'Pulling down my pants, Brer Fox,' said he.

"All this time, gracious honey, Brer Rabbit was putting on his spurs. When they got close to the girls' house where Brer Rabbit was to get off, Brer Fox made a sign for him to stop. Then Brer Rabbit slapped the spurs into Brer Fox's flanks—

and Brer Fox streaked across that ground, fast as could be. When they got to the house, all the girls were sitting on the piazza. Instead of stopping at the gate, Brer Rabbit rode right on by, he did, and then came galloping back down the road and up to the horse-rack, and hitched Brer Fox to it. Then he sauntered into the house, he did, and shook hands with the girls, and sat there smoking his cigar same as any town man. By and by he drew in a long puff and let it out in a cloud. Then he squared his shoulders back and hollered out loud:

" 'Ladies, didn't I tell you Brer Fox was the riding horse for our family? He's sorta losing his gait now, but I reckon I can fetch him round in a month or so,' said he.

"Then Brer Rabbit sorta grinned, he did, and the girls giggled, and went tripping daintily round the pony, praising his whiskers and his tail. And Brer Fox was hitched fast to the rack, and couldn't help himself.

"Is that all, Uncle Remus?" asked the little boy, as the old man paused.

"Well, that ain't exactly all, honey—but it wouldn't do to give out too much cloth for to make one pair of pants,' replied the old man sententiously.

# Cinderella

ONCE there was a rich man whose first wife died, leaving him with a small daughter. After some years the man married again, but his second wife was as proud as she was mean and loved no one except her own two ugly daughters. These girls, in turn, were jealous of the man's first child and soon made themselves the centre of the household, forcing the girl to become their servant. She had to scrub the floors and wash the dishes, shake out the heavy feather beds and, worst of all, get up before dawn each day to clean out the cinders in the hearth.

The poor girl slept in an attic under the roof on a sack full of straw. In wintertime, when the snow blew through the tiles and covered the sack like an eiderdown, she would lay herself down near the ashes and cinders in the kitchen hearth in order to keep warm. For this reason, and because her clothes were always dusty with the ashes from the fire, the two sisters used to call her Cinderella. In fact, they were jealous of her, for no matter how hard Cinderella worked nor how ragged her clothes were, she still looked far prettier than they.

One day the king's son gave a ball and invited all the fashionable people to it. Cinderella's stepmother and her daughters were invited along with the rest, and the ugly sisters set to work at once ordering elaborate gowns, petticoats and wigs for themselves. They made Cinderella starch the lace and pleat the frills, steam the velvet and iron the silk.

"I'm going to wear a red velvet gown with French trimmings," said the elder.

"I *think*," said the younger, "that I shall wear a gold-flowered blue bodice with my diamond stomacher, which is far from being the most ordinary one in the world."

They sent for the best hairdresser they could get to make up their wigs, and the most fashionable dressmaker to sew their new robes, and they bought beauty patches from the smartest shop in the city to stick on their faces.

While Cinderella helped them arrange their hair they teased her about the ball. "Wouldn't you like to go too?" they asked. "Oh, but of course you can't. Everyone there would laugh at the cinder dust on your dress."

Anyone other than Cinderella would have done their hair badly and ruined it, but she was a good, kind person and made them look as beautiful as she possibly could.

On the day of the ball the ugly sisters spent hours admiring themselves in the oval mirrors in their rooms. These could tip up or right down, and only the finest households had them. At last the hour of the ball drew near and they stepped into their coach and drove off to the palace in a cloud of red and blue flounces and frothy lace.

Cinderella watched them until they were out of sight. Then she went back to her seat by the fire and cried her heart out from loneliness and sorrow. Suddenly there was a tapping at the window, and a strange lady entered the kitchen. She had green eyes and a long cloak and she carried a small wand in her hand. She asked Cinderella what was the matter.

"I wish I could—I wish I could—" Cinderella was crying so hard that she could not finish her sentence.

"My dear, you wish you could go to the ball. Well, so you shall. A long time ago, when your mother was still alive, I became your fairy godmother. Now be a good girl and run into the garden and bring me a large, golden pumpkin."

Cinderella hurried into the garden and with the help of a lantern chose the finest pumpkin there and brought it to her godmother. That lady took a little silver knife out of her pocket and scooped out the centre of the pumpkin, leaving nothing but the rind. Then she struck it with her wand and it instantly turned into a fine coach. The girl had seen carriages with their grand ladies driving through the street when she was scrubbing the front steps, and she had wistfully seen her sisters riding haughtily off to the ball in their stylish coach, but she had never seen a coach like this, all covered in gold the colour of a pumpkin.

Next, her godmother asked her to look in the mousetrap in the pantry, where she found six mice, all alive. The fairy told Cinderella to lift up the little trap door, and as each mouse scuttled out, she gave it a tap with her wand and turned it into a fine horse with a long, flowing mane. In no time they were harnessed to the coach, and made a handsome team of six horses with beautiful, mouse-coloured grey coats.

"We still need a coachman," she said to Cinderella, who at once had an idea. "There's a rat trap in the shed," she cried. "I'll go and see if there's a rat in it that we could make into a coachman."

So she brought in the trap and inside it they found a stout rat with splendid whiskers, whom the fairy turned into a fat, jolly coachman with the smartest moustache you ever saw. After that she said to Cinderella, "Go into the garden again and you will find six lizards behind the watering can. Bring them to me."

Cinderella had no sooner done so than the godmother turned them into six footmen in livery who skipped up behind the coach and hung onto its straps as tightly as if they had done nothing else all their lives. Then the fairy turned to Cinderella and asked her if she was pleased.

"Oh, yes!" cried Cinderella. "But how can I go to the ball dressed in rags like this?"

Her godmother touched her once with the wand and her clothes were turned into a gown of Indian muslin edged with swansdown and pearls, silver and white like a summer's night. On her head lay a crown of starry flowers and on her hand she wore a ring of gold and precious stones. Finally the fairy changed the wooden clogs on her feet into slippers of spun glass lined with swansdown.

As Cinderella was just about to drive off in her coach and six, her godmother called out, "Remember to come back before midnight. If you stay a moment longer, the coach will be a pumpkin again, the horses mice,

the coachman a rat, the footmen lizards, and your clothes as ragged as before.''

Cinderella promised to leave the ball before twelve, and then away she drove, trembling with joy.

When they saw her step out of the coach the prince and all the court were struck dumb with admiration. The lords and ladies left off dancing and the violinists stopped playing, the better to admire Cinderella's beauty. Then, as the prince asked her to be his partner, the violinists took up their bows again and the music sounded more sweetly than ever before.

The king, the queen, and everyone present praised Cinderella's beauty and her graceful dancing, and wondered who she could be. But as the evening wore on and the prince danced with no one else, tongues began to wag behind fluttering fans,

matronly dowagers with marriageable daughters could not help looking askance beneath their heavily painted eyelids at this usurping stranger, while the slighted young misses themselves pouted increasingly at their less favoured partners—who were doing their own share of ogling the fair unknown. Cinderella and the prince, however, were oblivious of all this as they danced the evening away at what might have been their own private ball.

It is hard to say which of the two was the more transported—the girl, who seemed made of starlight, or the prince who held her luminous in his arms. Certain it is that the prince was so entranced by her that he did not even notice when supper was served and ate not a morsel of the rich banquet that had been prepared. Cinderella sat down by her sisters, politely offering them some of the

sugared oranges and lemons that the prince had given her. This flattered the two vain girls, who never recognized the lovely stranger as the girl they had left in the ashes at home.

Then the clock struck a quarter to midnight and Cinderella rose to go. She curtsied to the company and hurried away before anyone could even ask her name.

When she reached home, she told her fairy godmother what a wonderful time she had had and that the prince had begged her to attend the ball the following evening too. She was still thanking her godmother when she heard the sound of a coach pulling up, and ran to open the door for her sisters.

While Cinderella helped them undress and get ready for bed, they boasted to her about the lovely princess who had been so charming to them at the ball. Cinderella had to turn away so that they would not see her smiling.

Next evening the two sisters went to the ball again, and so did Cinderella, but this time she was dressed even more bewitchingly than before. The prince never left her side and the two of them danced and talked until they felt they had known each other all their lives. So lost were they in each other that Cinderella quite lost track of the time. As the clock began striking midnight, she started up and fled through the palace like a deer. The prince hurried after her, but he could not catch her. As she ran down the great staircase one of her glass slippers came off, and the prince picked it up and put it in his pocket.

The guards at the palace gate were asked if they had not seen a princess go out. They had seen nobody, they said, save for a young girl in rags, who looked like a kitchenmaid.

When the ugly sisters returned from the ball they told Cinderella that the prince had quite lost his heart to the mysterious princess who had vanished so suddenly, and that he had done nothing but gaze at her little glass slipper for the remainder of the evening.

The prince ordered that the slipper should be laid on a silk cushion and carried in state through the city, while his heralds read a proclamation that he would marry the girl whose foot the slipper fitted. It was to be tried on every unmarried lady, beginning at the top with the princesses and the duchesses.

The turn came for the ugly sisters to open their door to the royal messenger. The slipper was brought to the elder sister to try on, but push as she might, her foot was too big. So greedy was she to become a princess that she actually snipped off her big toe with a pair of scissors and managed to squeeze her foot into the slipper. But the royal messenger saw the blood through the glass and disqualified her.

Then the second sister tried on the slipper, but this time it was her heel that was too big. So she pared it down with a kitchen knife until the shoe fitted. However, she limped so badly that the messenger discovered her trick and disqualified her too.

Then Cinderella laughed and said, "Let *me* try on the slipper."

Despite her sisters' protests, the messenger kneeled down and slipped it on her foot. It fitted her as if it had been made of wax. Then Cinderella pulled out the other slipper from her pocket and put it on her other foot. The fairy godmother appeared at that moment and changed Cinderella's clothes into robes that were more magnificent than any she had worn before.

Then her two sisters recognized her as the beautiful lady at the ball, and they threw themselves at her feet and begged her pardon for their ill treatment of her. Cinderella kissed them and said she would forgive them gladly if they behaved to her like a sister, which they both promised they would from now on.

She was brought to the prince, who thought her more charming than ever, and a few days later they were married. Cinderella, who was as good as she was beautiful, found husbands for her sisters too, who were wealthy and kinder than they had any right to expect.

# The Little Tin Soldier

T HERE were once twenty-one tin soldiers, all brothers, who had been made out of the same old tin spoon. They wore splendid blue tunics with red trousers and stood stiffly at attention— *Shoulder arms! Eyes front!*—that's how they were. The very first words they ever heard when the lid was taken off the box in which they were lying, were "Tin soldiers!" It was a little boy who shouted this, for he had been given them for his birthday, and now he put them all on the table in a row.

Each soldier looked exactly like the others, except for one who was a little bit different. He had only one leg, because he was the last to be made and there was not enough tin for his second leg. Still, he stood up just as straight as the rest, and as it happens, it's this soldier that my story is about.

There were a lot of other toys on the table with the tin soldiers, because the small boy's little sister had a birthday on the same day and there were all kinds of presents for both of them from their mother and father, their grandparents, and all their aunts, uncles and cousins.

There was a round-eyed pink elephant with great white tusks jutting out over its drooping trunk, there was a teddy bear, a rabbit, a fluffy panda, a long-necked giraffe. A clown with bobbles dangling from his baggy costume and pointed hat was turning a somersault to amuse a dainty milkmaid who, carrying a pail and three-legged stool,

seemed more interested in ogling a dashing harlequin in his glittering tights of all the colours in the rainbow. A driver in goggles sat bolt upright at the wheel of a clockwork motor car. There was a bus, a fire engine and a miniature train. There was even a cardboard railway station, its signalman in his box holding a red flag to stop the train for the tiny passengers waiting on the platform.

But among more toys than the tin soldier had ever dreamed existed, the handsomest of all was a beautiful paper castle. You could see right into the rooms through some of its open windows. In front of it were some small trees dotted about a little lake made out of a gilt-framed mirror with three graceful swans swimming on its gleaming surface. Everything about it was pretty, but the prettiest of all was an enchanting little lady standing at the edge of the lake. She too

was cut out of paper, but she was wearing a billowing short dress of the finest muslin and a blue ribbon draped over her shoulder, with a glistening clasp at the centre nearly as big as her face. She was a ballet dancer, and had one arm outstretched and the other curved close to her head, and she had kicked one leg so far out behind her that the tin soldier didn't see it at first and could almost pretend that she had only one leg, like himself.

"That's the wife for me," he thought to himself. "She's so beautiful, poised on one foot. But she's very grand—she lives in a castle. I've got only a box that I share with all my brothers, and that's not good enough for her. Nevertheless, I must get to know her."

Later that evening all the tin soldiers went back into their box, except this one, who had hidden behind a snuffbox. After the people in the house had gone to bed the toys began to play games. They visited, they fought, they danced, and they made such a noise that the canary woke up and began singing. But the tin soldier just stood staunchly on his one leg. His eyes never left the little dancer for a moment.

Suddenly the clock struck midnight. Click! The lid of the snuffbox flew open and a little black goblin jumped up, like a Jack-in-the-box.

"Tin soldier!" cried the goblin. "Will you please keep your eyes to yourself!" But the tin soldier did not answer. He just went on looking at the little dancer.

"All right—you wait until tomorrow!" the goblin exclaimed.

When tomorrow came the children put the tin soldier on the window sill, and whether it was the goblin or the wind that did it, the soldier fell out headlong through the open window, landing upside down on his helmet, with his leg sticking straight up in the air and his bayonet jammed in between the paving stones.

The little boy came down to look for him, but although he very nearly trod on him, he never saw him. If only the tin soldier had called out, "Here I am!" the boy would have found him. But he did not think a soldier in uniform ought to shout.

Then it began to rain, more and more heavily. People hurried past sheltering under umbrellas and with no one giving so much as a thought to the little tin soldier jammed upside down on the pavement with the rain beating relentlessly against his face and unprotected uniform.

When the rain stopped, leaving the street full of puddles, two little boys came by. "Oh, look!" said one of them. "There's a tin soldier. Let's send him for a sail." So they made a boat out of some paper, put the tin soldier in it, and away he sailed down the gutter, with the two boys running beside him and shouting. The paper boat bobbed up and down and whirled around so fast that the tin soldier became quite giddy. But

he kept upright and never moved a muscle. He looked straight ahead, still shouldering arms.

Suddenly the boat drifted into a broad drain, and it became quite dark. "I wonder where I'm going now," thought the soldier. "If only the little lady was here with me, I wouldn't mind if it were twice as dark!"

Just then a large water rat appeared, who lived in the drain. "Where's your passport?" asked the rat. "Now then, show me your passport!"

But the tin soldier just went on looking straight ahead, clutching his gun tightly. The boat rushed on and the rat hurried after it shouting, "Stop him! Stop him!" to the sticks and straws.

The current grew stronger and stronger and the tin soldier could already see daylight ahead, where the drain ended. But he could also hear a roaring sound that brought terror into his heart. Just imagine—where the drain ended it plunged straight out into a large canal. That was as dangerous for him as plunging over Niagara Falls would be for us.

By now he was going so fast that there was no stopping the boat. It dashed out, with the tin soldier holding himself as stiffly as he could, spun round three or four times, and filled with water. The tin soldier was up to his neck in it. The boat sank deeper and deeper as its paper grew more and more soaked. At last the water closed over the tin soldier's head. He thought of the pretty little dancer he would never see again, and an old song rang in his ears:

*"Go onward, brave soldier!*
*Face death without fear!"*

At this moment the paper fell to pieces and the tin soldier sank straight through—but was instantly swallowed by a large fish. It was even darker inside the fish's stomach than it had been inside the drain, and terribly cramped.

The fish darted about, twisting and turn-

ing in a most terrifying manner. Then at last it lay quite still, and broad daylight flashed through it. Someone called out, "A tin soldier!" For the fish had been caught, taken to market and sold, and brought into this kitchen, where the cook cut it open with a big knife. She picked up the soldier and carried him into the nursery, where everyone wanted to see this extraordinary man who had been travelling about inside a fish. They set him up on the table, and there—well, what wonderful things can happen!

The tin soldier found himself in exactly the same room he had been in before. There they were—the same children, the same toys on the table, the same beautiful paper castle with the pretty little dancer who still stood on one leg and kept the other one high in the air. She too had never moved. This touched the tin soldier, who could have wept for love of her, except that he felt soldiers ought not to weep. He looked at her and she looked at him, but neither of them so much as murmured a single word.

Suddenly one of the small boys picked up the soldier and threw him straight into the fire. He had no real reason for doing this— of course the bad goblin was behind it all.

The tin soldier stood completely wrapped in flames. The heat that he felt was tremendous, but whether it came from the fire or from the love in his heart he did not know. His bright blue and red colours were gone, but no one could tell whether this was as a result of his rough voyage or his grief. He looked at the little lady, she looked at him, and he could feel that he was melting, but he stood stiffly upright, still shouldering arms.

Then someone opened the nursery door. The draught caught the dancer and she flew like a bird right into the fire to the tin soldier. She flared up for a second and was gone. The tin soldier was melted down to a lump and when the maid cleared out the ashes next morning, she found him in the shape of a little tin heart. And all that was left of the dancer was a little tin clasp that was burned as black as coal.

# Rapunzel

ONCE upon a time a man and his wife lived in a small house which lay close to a splendid garden that belonged to a witch. From their windows they could see rare herbs and flowers growing in the garden, but they never dared to pick any for they knew that if they did they would fall into the witch's power.

One day, however, the wife fell ill with a fever and it seemed certain that she would die. In her sickness she longed for one thing only: the leaves of a herb called rampion, which grew in the witch's garden. Her husband, who loved her dearly, was ready to risk anything to save his wife and so, at

dusk, he climbed over the witch's garden wall. He picked some of the leaves and returned safely with them to his wife, who ate them and recovered her strength. It was not long, however, before she fell ill again, and this time it was the root of the herb she wanted.

At dusk the husband again climbed over the wall, and tried to pull the herb up by its roots. Suddenly he felt a burning pain in his hands, and looking up, he saw the witch standing in front of him.

"A curse on you," she cried, "for stealing the rampion from my garden!"

"My wife is ill, and will die without your

herb!" pleaded the man, but the witch had no mercy.

"Go," she said, "but in exchange for the rampion you have stolen, I shall take your first-born child. I shall come and collect it on the day that it is born."

Not long afterwards a daughter was born to the couple, and no sooner had she opened her eyes to the world than the witch appeared to claim her as she had declared she would. In their rejoicing at the birth of the child they had so ardently awaited, the couple had pushed to the back of their minds the harsh demand the witch had made of the husband, and they begged her now to let them keep their small daughter. But neither tears nor entreaty had any effect on the merciless witch who, impatient to be off, picked up the child and carried her ruthlessly away. From the start she called her Rapunzel, which is another name for rampion.

Years passed and Rapunzel grew up to be the loveliest creature in the world. When she was twelve the witch locked her into a tower in the depths of a forest surrounded by mountains. The tower had neither stairs nor door, and the only way into it was through Rapunzel's window, high up in the wall. When the witch wanted to visit her she would call up:

*"Rapunzel, Rapunzel,*
*Let down your hair."*

The girl had wonderfully long golden hair which she would twist into a thick plait and wind around the window bar, so that it dropped clear down to the ground and the witch could use it as a rope to climb up.

A prince who had lost his way in the forest came riding past the tower one evening. As he drew near he heard the loveliest voice he had ever heard singing, and he stopped to listen. It was Rapunzel, singing to herself in her loneliness. Then he heard the witch's voice call up:

> *"Rapunzel, Rapunzel,*
> *Let down your hair."*

He saw thick coils of golden hair let down from the tiny window. The witch climbed up and disappeared from view. The prince was determined to see the girl who sang so sweetly, so he waited until the witch had gone, and then he called up:

> *"Rapunzel, Rapunzel,*
> *Let down your hair."*

At once the golden rope swung down the tower wall to him, and he climbed up it. As soon as he saw Rapunzel's beauty he fell in love with her, and he asked her to become his wife. Rapunzel, who had never seen anyone but the old witch, was delighted by this handsome young man, and agreed to escape with him. She said:

"Every time you come to see me you must bring a skein of silk and I will plait it into a ladder as thick as my hair and then we can climb down and ride away together."

The prince came to see her every evening because the witch visited her during the daytime. The day of their escape was drawing near when Rapunzel, who could think of nothing but her prince, said dreamily to the witch:

"Why is it, good dame, that you are so much heavier to pull up than my prince?"

Thus the witch learned that Rapunzel had deceived her, and she flew into a rage. She cut off Rapunzel's long hair and tied it to the window bars. Then she carried the girl to a distant valley and left her there alone to live in misery.

That evening, the prince came and called to his beloved as usual. Her hair came tumbling down to him, and he climbed up into the tower. But this time it was the witch who pulled him in, cursing him as she did so.

"She is gone!" she cried. "You will never see her again!" With that she threw the young man out of the window, into the forest below. He fell into a thicket of briars, and the thorns scratched his eyes and blinded him. He wandered, blind and sad, through the forests and over the mountains, weeping for his beloved.

One day at last he came to the valley where Rapunzel was living. As soon as she saw him she ran to him, weeping, and her tears fell on his eyes and healed them, so that he could see again, as well as ever.

Then the prince took Rapunzel to his kingdom, where they married and lived the rest of their lives in complete happiness.

# Foolish Jim & Clever James

ONCE there was a fellow whom every-one called Foolish Jim because he was so contrary. In the middle of summer he would light a big fire in the house and in the winter he would shiver over a cold grate.

He would cook a chicken and give it to his horse to eat, and then eat oats for his own dinner. He would water his vegetable patch when it was raining and leave it to shrivel under the sun. At night he would spread a

mattress over the bed and lie down to sleep on the hard floor. Everything he did in fact was just plain topsy-turvy. The king heard about his curious ways and thought he would have some fun. So Jim was sent for.

"Can you answer riddles?" asked the king.

"Yes," said Foolish Jim.

"If you can answer this one, you can marry my daughter," said the king, who didn't think Jim could possibly answer a riddle. "But you have only three guesses, and if you fail your head will be chopped off. Fifty men have lost their lives already."

"I can answer it," said Foolish Jim.

"What begins on four legs, proceeds on

two legs, and ends up with three legs?" asked the king. Jim said he would have to go home to think up the answer.

Now Jim had an evil neighbour who wanted Jim's horse, which was a good one. He left a basket of poisoned pies on the bridge that Jim would cross on his way back from the palace, and went away feeling sure Jim would eat the pies and die so that he could take his horse.

When Jim saw the pies he got down from his horse intending to eat them. Then he began to wonder why anyone would leave such good pies there and go away, instead of eating them himself. So he gave the pies to his horse, who immediately dropped dead.

"What a good thing I didn't eat them," he thought. He threw the horse's body into the river, and as it floated downstream, three crows alighted on it and began to peck at the flesh.

Jim went straight back to the king. "The answer," he said, "is that a man first crawls on all fours, then walks on two legs when he's grown up, and leans on a stick when he is old—which makes three."

The king was astonished. "My daughter is yours," he said.

"May I ask you a riddle now?" said Jim. Now the king thought himself so clever that he could answer any riddle, so he replied, "If I cannot answer it, my whole kingdom is yours."

"Here it is," said Jim. "A dead being passes along with three live ones riding it and feeding on it. It does not touch the land, neither is it in the sky."

The king puzzled and puzzled. He answered this and that, but in the end he had to give up.

Jim said, "My horse died as I was coming here, and I threw it in the river. Three crows sat on it and began to eat it. It didn't touch the land, neither was it in the sky."

The king was even more amazed at Foolish Jim's cleverness, and had to give him his crown and kingdom. And from then on, Foolish Jim was known as Clever James.

# The Ugly Duckling

IT was summertime and a mother duck was sitting on her eggs. She had hidden her nest at the far end of a pond, among the waterweeds that grew there. She was longing for her little ducklings to hatch out for she was lonely. Hardly anyone bothered to visit her; the other ducks preferred to swim about in the pond rather than sit under a dock leaf quacking with her.

At last the eggs cracked open one after the other. "Peep! Peep!" the little ducklings said, sticking their heads out of the shells.

"Quack! Quack!" said the mother duck, and then the little ones scuttled out as quickly as they could, and began peering under leaves and twigs.

"Oh, how big the world is!" said the ducklings. And it certainly was much bigger than the eggs that they had been lying in.

"Do you imagine that this is the whole world?" the mother duck said. "Why, it goes a long way past the other side of the garden, right to the edge of the field, but I've never been as far as that." She got up from her nest, thinking that all the eggs had been hatched. But then she noticed that there was still one egg left, the largest one of all. She sat down again.

At last the big egg cracked. There was a gentle "Peep! Peep!" from the young one as he fell out, looking so large and ugly. The mother duck looked at him and said, "My! What a big duckling he is! None of the others looked a bit like that."

Then she plopped down into the water. "Quack! Quack!" she called to the ducklings, and one after the other they all jumped in. The water closed over their heads, but in a moment they had popped up again and were floating along beautifully.

"Look how well they use their legs," the mother duck said proudly, nodding at the ugly grey one among them, who was swimming along as strongly as the rest. "Now let me show you the world and introduce you to the barnyard. But keep close to me so that nobody steps on you; and watch out for the cat."

There was a lot of noise going on in the farmyard, for two families were fighting for an eel's head, and in the end it was the cat that got it. The other ducks in the yard stared at the new arrivals and said loudly, "What do we want more ducks for? Ugh! What a sight that duckling is! We can't possibly put up with him!" And one duck immediately waddled up to the duckling and bit him in the neck.

"He's so awkward and peculiar," they all said. "We'll just have to squash him."

"Not on your life!" said the duckling's mother. "He's not handsome but he's good-tempered and he can swim just as well as the others. The trouble with him was that he lay too long in the egg—that's why he's that peculiar shape. Anyhow, he's a drake, so it doesn't matter if he isn't handsome. He looks as if he'll be strong one day, though."

"Your ducklings are charming, my dear," said an old, important-looking duck, and so they were allowed to make themselves at home in the farmyard. But the poor duckling who was so ugly was pecked and jostled and teased by every fowl in the barnyard. The duckling didn't know where to turn and was terribly unhappy.

Things grew worse and worse as the days went on; even his brothers and sisters began saying, "If only the cat would get you, you clumsy great goof!" until the mother duck herself wished he were far away.

One day, when the girl who fed the

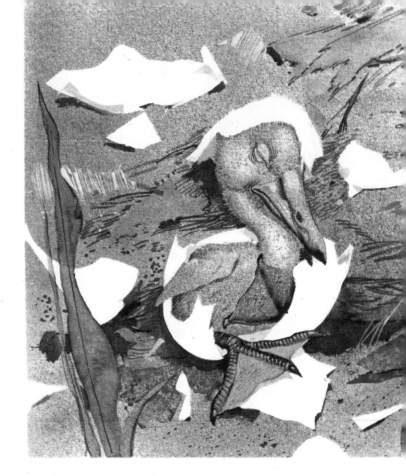

poultry kicked at the duckling with her foot, he ran away. He fluttered over the hedge, and the little birds clustered there grew frightened and flew into the air. "That's because I am so ugly," thought the duckling, and ran away even farther. At night he came to the great marsh where the wild ducks lived and lay there, tired and dejected.

In the morning the wild ducks flew up to look at him. "Who are you?" they asked. "What a scarecrow you are! But that doesn't matter as long as you don't marry into our family." Poor thing! He wasn't dreaming of getting married; all he wanted was to stay quietly among the rushes. But even this he was not allowed to do, for some men came with guns and shot the wild ducks dead, and big dogs broke through the rushes and picked them up in their mouths. One dog pushed its muzzle right down to the duckling, crouching in the rushes. Then it bared its teeth and went off without touching him.

"I'm so ugly that even the dog won't bite me," he thought, and hurried away from the marsh as fast as he could.

It was a cold, bleak day, and he had never been so far before nor felt so lost and lonely.

Towards evening he came to a poor little

cottage, so rickety that it hardly knew which way to fall and therefore stayed upright. He slipped into the house through a crack in the door, to shelter from the wind.

An old woman lived there with her cat and her hen. The cat could purr very loudly and the hen was a good layer, and the woman loved them like her own children. When she saw the duckling she was glad, for she hoped it too might lay eggs for her.

The hen, who was very proud of herself, said, "Can you lay eggs?" and the duckling replied, "No."

The cat asked, "Can you purr?" and again the duckling had to say, "No."

"Well, then, you're no use here," they both said, and he was made to sit in the corner. Suddenly he remembered the fresh

air and the sunshine, and he felt a great longing to swim in the water.

"It would be so lovely to duck my head down under the water and dive to the bottom," the duckling told the cat.

"You must be crazy," she replied.

"I think I'll go out into the wide world again," said the duckling.

"Yes, do," said the hen and the cat.

And so the duckling went off. He swam in the lake; he dived down to the bottom but still he could not make friends with any of the other creatures, because he was so ugly.

Then autumn came. The leaves in the wood turned yellow and brown, the wind carried them off the branches and danced them about, while the sky took on a frosty look. The clouds were heavy with rain and

sleet, and the raven who perched on the fence kept squawking, "Ow! Ow!" because he felt so cold.

One evening, when there was a lovely sunset, a flock of large, handsome birds appeared on the lake. The duckling had never seen such beautiful birds; they were shining white and had long, graceful necks. They gave a weird cry, spread out their great wings, and flew from this cold country to warmer lands and open lakes.

They rose high and the ugly little duckling felt strange as he watched them. He turned round and round in the water like a wheel, and craned his neck after them, letting out a cry so shrill that it quite frightened him. Ah! He could never forget those beautiful, fortunate birds; and directly they disappeared from his sight he dived under the water, for he was almost beside himself with excitement. He did not know what the birds were called, nor where they were flying to, and yet they were dearer to him than anything he had ever known. Yet he did not envy them in the least, for he never dreamed he could be part of such loveliness.

It was a very cold winter. The duckling had to keep swimming about in the water to stop it freezing under him. But every night the pool he was swimming in grew smaller and smaller; the ice froze so hard that it cracked and froze again. The duckling had to keep his feet moving all the time to stop the ice from closing in. At last he grew faint with exhaustion, and lay still. Finally, he froze fast in the ice.

Early next morning a farmer came by and saw him. He broke the ice around him with a stick, and carried him home to his wife. And there she revived the duckling.

The children wanted to play with him, but he was afraid of them and flew in panic right into the milk bowl, so that the milk splashed all over the counter. The woman screamed and clapped her hands in the air, and then he flew into the butter tub and from there into the flour bin and out again.

What a sight he looked! The woman screamed again and hit at him with the poker, while the children ran around trying to catch him, laughing and shouting. It was a good thing that the door was open; the duckling darted out into the bushes and sank down exhausted into the soft snow.

It would be too sad a story to describe all the misery the poor duckling went through during that hard, cold winter. He was sheltering among the reeds in the marsh when the sun at last began to get warmer and the days lighter. Spring had arrived.

Suddenly he felt he had to try his wings; they were stronger than before, and they carried him higher. Almost before he realized it, he found himself in a garden with apple trees in blossom and sweet-smelling lilac dangling over the stream. Everything here was lovely and soft and fresh. Then three beautiful white swans came in sight, floating lightly on the water. The duckling recognized them and was overcome with a feeling of sadness.

"I will fly across to those royal birds," he thought. "They will peck me to death because I am so ugly. But it's better to be killed by them than be pecked and nipped by the other creatures and go through another terrible winter." As he swam over to them, the birds came hurrying towards him, "Kill me!" cried the duckling, and bowed his head to the water, awaiting death. But what did he see there in the clear stream? It was a reflection of himself, but he was no longer a clumsy, grey, ugly bird—no, he was

himself a graceful long-necked swan!

You see, it doesn't matter being born in a duck's nest as long as you are hatched from a swan's egg.

The three great swans swam round and round, stroking him with their beaks. Some little children came into the garden and threw bread into the water. "There's a new swan!" they cried. "It's the prettiest of them all—so young and handsome!" And the older swans bowed to him. He ruffled his feathers, raised his lovely neck, and was touched to his heart by all that had happened to him. "I never dreamed of so much happiness, when I was the ugly duckling," he thought to himself.

# The Sleeping Beauty

ONCE upon a time there were a king and a queen who were unhappy because they had no children. They had been married a long time and had almost given up hope when at last their dearest wish came true with the birth of a most beautiful baby girl. Their joy was so great that no cost was spared in the preparations for the splendid christening to which the king and queen invited all the fairies in the kingdom. All, that is, except one. There were thirteen fairies in the domain, but actually only twelve had been invited because no one knew exactly where the thirteenth was to be found; when last heard of some time ago she was living alone in an isolated hamlet in some distant part of the realm. Not that any great pains had been taken to look for her. Nobody liked her very much anyway; she was always inclined to be crochety and quarrelsome and was always picking on the other fairies, probably because they were all younger and prettier than she was.

Since the custom, then as now, was to make gifts to the baby on its christening day, the twelve fairies were asked to be godmothers, with no doubt in anyone's mind that they would bestow every manner of good fortune on the little princess.

After the christening ceremony, all the guests proceeded to the king's castle where a great feast awaited them in the magnificent banqueting hall. Each fairy's place was set

with elaborate plates and tableware of the finest gold, with goblets of the purest crystal, made especially in their honour. But just as everyone was about to be seated, the thirteenth fairy appeared in a rush of rage at having been overlooked. The king at once ordered a place to be set for her, but to his embarrassment there were golden appointments only for the invited fairies, so the new arrival had to be served from the same dishes as the rest of the company, which only made her glower all the more with menace.

Fearing some mischief was brewing, the youngest fairy hid herself behind the tapestry hangings so that she would be the last to announce her gift and could undo whatever harm the old fairy was plotting.

Then the fairies began to make their gifts to the little princess. The first gave her beauty, the second goodness, the third gracefulness, the fourth made her a perfect dancer, the fifth gave her a lovely singing voice, and the sixth, the skill to play every musical instrument in the world perfectly. In short, they gave her everything one could wish for in life.

Then came the old fairy's turn. Angrily, she stepped up to the princess's cradle and cried out with jealous spite, "When you are fifteen you will prick your finger with a spindle and fall lifeless to the ground!"

Then she turned around and left the hall.

At this terrible curse everyone trembled and began to weep. But at that instant the youngest fairy stepped out of her hiding place.

"Take heart," she said to the king and queen, "your daughter shall not die. It is true that I have not the power to undo the envious fairy's spell completely. The princess will indeed prick her finger with a spindle when she is fifteen. But instead of dying, she will only fall into a deep sleep that will last a hundred years, and when that time has passed, a king's son will come and waken her."

The king, hoping to save his daughter from the old fairy's spell, immediately ordered that every spindle and every spinning wheel in the country should be burned.

All the good wishes of the first fairies came true. The princess grew into a young girl of such beauty, goodness, and grace as had never been seen before. She had just become fifteen when one afternoon she was playing a game of hide-and-seek with the other boys and girls in the castle. It was her turn to hide, and she ran into the farthest end of the courtyard, where there were several doors that led into a cluster of towers which had been shut up for many years. She found herself in front of a little door she had never noticed before, and pushed it open. She climbed the winding stairs, up and up, into a narrow tower. At length she reached a little room at the top, and there she found an old woman sitting at a spinning wheel, with the wheel whirring round and the flax twirling on the spindle.

"What are you doing?" asked the princess, who had never, of course, seen such a sight before.

"I am spinning," replied the old woman, who obviously had not heard of the king's

decree that every spinning wheel in the land should be destroyed, and did not know who her visitor was. "Sometimes I spin flax into linen, sometimes I spin a sheep's fleece into wool. Sometimes I even spin gold into thread for fine ladies to sew with."

"Is it difficult?" asked the princess.

"Yes, at first it is," the old woman replied.

"Let me try, please!" the princess begged, and the old woman handed her the spindle and the thread. No sooner had she taken the spindle than its point pricked her hand and she immediately fell to the ground in a swoon. The curse of the wicked old fairy had come true.

The old woman, terrified, cried out for help, and people came running from all parts of the castle. They tried to bring the princess round by throwing water on her face, loosening her gown, and holding smelling salts under her nose, but nothing worked.

Realizing that the spell had begun and must run its course, the king ordered his daughter to be carried to her bedchamber and laid on a bedspread embroidered with gold and silver, to sleep in peace until the appointed hundred years had passed.

When the accident happened the good fairy who had saved the princess's life by changing the curse from one of death to one of deep sleep, was in the kingdom of Matakin, twelve thousand leagues away. She was told about it instantly by a dwarf who had a pair of seven-league boots—which enabled him to cover seven leagues in each stride. The fairy left immediately in a chariot of fire drawn by six dragons, and arrived at the king's palace in less than an hour.

As she walked through the palace she brushed every living thing in it with her

wand, except the king and queen. As she touched them, they fell asleep—ministers, governesses, clerks, maids of honour, soldiers, cowherds, footmen, pages. She also touched the horses in the stable, the cows and the chickens, the doves and the mice, and Puff, the princess's puppy, who had curled up beside her on her bed. The spits in the fireplace stopped turning and the cook, who was about to box the kitchen boy's ears for tasting the gravy, fell asleep with his arm still raised. The kitchenmaid, who was

plucking a fowl held firmly on her lap, slumbered with her hands still among its feathers. Outside in the courtyard the wind stopped blowing and in the gardens the flowers closed their petals and prepared for their long night.

Then the king and queen kissed their beloved daughter and sadly left the castle for ever.

Within a quarter of an hour a forest of trees and briars had grown up around its walls, so thickly intertwined that no one could pass through them and disturb the princess as she slept. The topmost turrets of the castle could barely be seen above the mass of greenery. The fairy had done her work quickly and well.

Ninety-nine summers and ninety-nine winters had passed when one fine day the son of the reigning king—who was of quite another family from that of the sleeping princess—was hunting in the forest. He caught sight of the distant turrets and asked his men what they were. Some told him that they believed it was a ruin haunted by spirits, others that witches and sorcerers used it at nights. Most of them seemed to think it was a castle that belonged to an ogre, who was the only creature who was able to make his way through the tough, dense, impenetrable forest.

Finally, an old peasant stepped forward and said:

"May it please your highness, more than fifty years ago I heard my father say that *his* grandfather told him there was a castle in this forest in which the most beautiful princess ever born was lying asleep. She was under a spell and it is said that she could be awakened only by a king's son."

The prince's heart was set on fire by these words. Impatient to discover the truth for himself, he drew his sword and advanced towards the briars. The metal flashed in the sunlight as he struck it into the deepest knot of thorns. To his surprise it gave way easily— he had only to touch the branches for them to fall apart and allow a passage large enough to let him and his horse through. What surprised him even more was that as soon as he had passed through the briars they closed again behind him, cutting his followers off.

Alone, he advanced through the first courtyard, which was filled with horses and men whom at first he thought were dead. Then he realized that they were all asleep and breathing peacefully. The clatter of his horse's hoofs echoed in the stillness, but the pigeons on the battlements slept as soundly

as the guards leaning on their weapons.

He entered another marble courtyard, where he left his horse while he climbed the great staircase lined with snoring guards. He passed through several chambers filled with lords and ladies all fast asleep, some sitting, others standing up. Finally, he came to a room where the pale light filtered through draperies finespun as maidenhair onto a bedecked bed on which lay a sleeping girl more ravishing than any he had ever beheld.

Trembling, the prince approached the bed and fell on his knees beside it, gazing at the princess. The tapering fingers of her hand rested lightly on a puppy curled up sleeping in the crook of her arm. A faint smile played about her lips as if a sweet dream contented her as she slept. At last the prince bent over the princess and kissed her gently on the forehead. And now the enchantment was at an end. At the touch of his lips the princess awoke. "I have waited for you so long," she said, smiling at the prince.

Together they walked through the castle and wherever they went the people woke up around them. The spits in the fireplace began to turn again, the kitchenmaid began plucking the fowl in her lap, while the cook at last gave the kitchen boy the box on the ears that had waited a hundred years. All the court awoke and everyone set about their duties again.

The prince and the princess went into the great hall, where a delicious supper was served to them. While they ate, the princess's minstrels played from the gallery above, and the prince noticed that they were using instruments that had long ceased to be played everywhere else. However, their tunes gave great pleasure, although none of them had been heard for a hundred years.

The prince and the princess, who were falling more deeply in love with every minute that passed, were married as soon as supper was over. And then the merriment and rejoicing, the feasting and music-making began all over again, for after so long a sleep the time seemed short indeed.

# Hansel & Gretel

ONCE upon a time a poor woodcutter lived on the edge of a forest with his wife and two children. The boy was called Hansel and the girl Gretel. They never had enough to eat, and as time went by, the whole country ran short of food and the family began to starve. At last, all they had to eat were a few shrivelled apples. There was not even so much as a crumb of bread left in the house.

That night, when the woodcutter went to bed, he said to his wife, who was the children's stepmother:

"What is to become of us all? How can we live without food?"

"We can't," she said. "Tomorrow morning we must take the children into the farthest part of the forest and leave them there while we go and collect wood to sell. They will never be able to find their way home again and we shall only have ourselves to find food for."

"*No*, wife!" protested the woodcutter. "I can't leave my own children in the forest to be eaten by wild beasts."

"If you don't all four of us will die of hunger, and you may just as well go and start making our coffins now." And being a mean and nagging woman, she went on arguing until at last he reluctantly agreed to her heartless plan.

Now Hansel and Gretel had not been able to go to sleep because they were still so hungry, and they overheard what their stepmother said. Gretel was very frightened and began to cry. "We're going to die, Hansel!" she wept.

"Don't cry, Gretel, I'll find a way to help us," Hansel reassured her.

He waited until his father and stepmother had gone to sleep and then he got out of bed, put on his clothes, opened the door, and slipped out of the house. The moon was shining brightly and the white pebbles that lay in front of the house glittered like pieces of silver. Hansel bent down and filled his coat and trouser pockets with them. Then he went back to Gretel, who was still awake.

"Don't worry, little sister," he said, hugging her tight. "I'll see to it that we don't get lost in the forest." And they went to sleep with their arms around each other.

At dawn the stepmother came in and shook them awake. "Get up, you lazybones —we are all going into the forest to fetch wood."

She gave each of them two apples. "That's for your lunch," she said sourly. "It's all you get today."

Gretel carried the apples in her apron, for Hansel had his pockets full of the pebbles. After they had walked a little while Hansel began to lag behind and kept looking back at the house.

His father noticed this. "Why are you always looking behind you?" he asked Hansel. "You'll stumble and fall if you don't take more care."

"I'm just looking at my white kitten, father," said Hansel quickly. "It's sitting on the roof and waving goodbye to me like it always does."

"You fool!" scolded his stepmother. "That isn't your kitten, that's the sun shining on the chimney."

But in fact Hansel was laying a trail of pebbles on the path behind them.

When they had reached the middle of the forest the father said, "We shall light a big fire here. You can keep it alight with the dry sticks on the ground." And when they had collected a large heap of these and the flames began to take a good hold, he told them:

"Now lie down by the fire, children, and

rest. Your mother and I are going farther into the forest to cut more wood. When we have finished, we shall come back and fetch you."

So Hansel and Gretel sat down near the fire and waited. They stoked it and waited. At lunchtime they ate their apples. They could hear the sound of an axe in the distance and thought it was their father felling trees. But it was not an axe that they heard; it was a branch the wind was blowing against a tree. They talked a little at first to cheer each other up, but after they had waited a very long time their eyelids grew heavier and heavier. Finally, huddled together side by side, they both fell fast asleep.

When they woke up it was completely dark and the fire had gone out completely.

"We shall never find our way out of this wood again," cried Gretel, beginning to weep.

"Wait," said Hansel. "The moon will be up soon and then we shall be able to see again."

Once the moon had risen he took his sister by the hand and followed the track of pebbles, which shone like silver coins in the moonlight, leading them all the way back to their parents' house. They knocked at the door, and when the woman opened it and saw Hansel and Gretel, she pretended that she had been expecting to see them.

"You naughty children," she scolded, "why did you sleep so long in the forest?

We began to think you were never coming home."

But their father was really glad to see them and hugged them close, for he had bitterly regretted leaving them behind.

Not long afterwards there was another great famine in the country, and once again there was no more food in the woodcutter's house. That night the hungry children heard their stepmother say:

"It's no good—the children will have to go. There's not enough food left to feed all of us."

Again the father argued and pleaded with her and again she insisted on getting her way in the end.

When his parents had gone to sleep, Hansel got out of bed and tried, as he had done before, to fill his pockets with pebbles. But this time his stepmother had bolted the door and he could not get out. So he returned to Gretel and tried to comfort her. "Don't worry," he reassured her. "Sleep well now for God will take care of us later."

Next morning the woman woke the children at dawn, gave them each a crust of bread for lunch, and told them they were going to collect wood in the forest again.

On the way there Hansel kept looking back at the house, and his father asked him why he was so slow.

"I'm looking at my little pigeon sitting on the roof," he answered.

"That isn't your pigeon, idiot—that's the sun shining on the chimney," said the woman.

But in reality Hansel was crumbling up the bread in his pocket and dropping it on the ground to mark the trail.

This time they went even deeper into the forest than before. Again the parents lit a big fire and told the children to sit by it and wait while they went to cut wood. "In the evening we shall come back and fetch you," the stepmother told Hansel and Gretel.

At midday Gretel shared her bread with Hansel, for he had strewn all his along the trail. Then they fell asleep, and the sun set while they were still sleeping. When they awoke it was quite dark. Gretel began to cry, and Hansel comforted her by saying:

"The moon will be up soon, Gretel, and then we shall see the breadcrumbs I scattered on the path. They will show us the way back to the house like the pebbles did before."

But when the moon had risen there were no breadcrumbs to be seen, because the birds and insects in the forest had eaten them all up.

"Never mind," Hansel said bravely to Gretel. "We shall just have to find our own way out."

By the third morning they realized that they were completely lost. They seemed to be wandering in circles that led deeper and deeper into the forest. Feeling tired and hungry and frightened, they sat down on a log and wondered what to do next. Suddenly they realized that a beautiful little snow-white bird was sitting on a branch above their heads, singing most sweetly. It seemed to be singing to them, encouraging them not to despair. Then it fluttered a little way off and seemed to be waiting for them. They rose and kept following it through the trees until they came to a little house in a clearing. It was no ordinary house, for its walls were built of honey bread and nuts, its roof was tiled with sugar cakes, and its windows were made of peppermint sticks.

"Now we can eat all we want," shouted Hansel, and he and Gretel began pulling off pieces of the roof and walls, and stuffing them into their mouths.

Then a voice called from inside:

*"Nibble, nibble, little mouse,*
*Who is nibbling at my house?"*

*"The wind, the wind,*
*The heaven-born wind,"*

the children called back gaily with their mouths crammed full.

They had eaten a big chunk of the roof and were pulling out the windowpanes so that they could lick them more easily when suddenly the door of the house opened and

an old woman came hobbling out, leaning heavily on a crutch. The children shrank back in terror, but instead of scolding them, she smiled at them and said sweetly:

"My dears, however did you find your way here? Come inside and I will give you better food than this. Don't be afraid—no harm will come to you."

She took the children's hands and led them into the kitchen, where a wonderful meal had already been prepared. On the table stood steaming hot pancakes, with syrup and apples and nuts. When they had eaten their fill, the old woman led them to a room with two cosy little white beds in it. Hansel and Gretel fell asleep that night thinking they must surely have reached heaven.

But the old woman was only pretending to be friendly. In reality she was an evil witch, whose favourite food was little children. She had built the house of sugar and spice to entice children to visit her, and once they were in her power she killed them, cooked them, and ate them. The witch had red eyes and could hardly see at all, but she could smell as well as a dog or a wolf. When she had smelled Hansel and Gretel a long way off, she had laughed to herself at the prospect of such a tasty dish.

At daybreak next day she went to the

room where the children were sleeping peacefully, snatched up Hansel, and carried him, kicking and struggling, to the yard outside, where she locked him in a cage. Then she shook Gretel awake.

"Get up, you lazy girl!" she shouted. "Fetch some water from the well in the yard to cook your brother something good. I am going to fatten him up, and when he is fat enough, I shall eat him."

Gretel was terrified, but she had to do as she was told. Every day she cleaned the house and helped the witch cook huge meals for Hansel, while she herself was only allowed to eat the scrapings from the bottom of the pot.

Every morning the old witch hobbled out to the yard and cried out shrilly, "Hansel, stick your little finger through the bars so that I can feel how very nice and fat you're getting."

But Hansel always slipped a chicken bone through the bars instead, and the witch, who could hardly see at all, pinched it and couldn't understand why Hansel never grew any fatter.

When a month had gone by and Hansel was still as thin as ever, despite all the good food she had given him, the old witch could wait no longer.

"Go to the well," she ordered Gretel, "and fetch me a bucket of water. Whether Hansel is fat or thin, I'm going to boil him in a pot and eat him for my lunch tomorrow."

Poor Gretel wept and begged the witch not to do it. "If only the wild beasts in the forest had eaten us, then at least we would have died together. Dear God, help us!" she cried.

"Hold your tongue!" shouted the witch. "Crying won't help you."

Early the next morning Gretel had to go out and gather wood for the fire and set the big pot of water on the stove to boil. She began to cry again when she thought what the water was to be used for.

"First we'll bake the bread," said the witch. "I have kneaded the dough and put it on the shelf to rise. Open the oven door and tell me if it's hot enough for me to put the bread in to bake."

And she pushed Gretel towards the oven, intending to push her into it and bake her so that she could eat her as well as Hansel. But Gretel had guessed her plan.

"I don't know how to tell if the oven is hot enough. Will you show me, please?" she asked.

"You silly goose, *this* is how you do it," said the witch impatiently, and she opened the oven door wide and bent over to feel the heat. Gretel gave her a push that toppled her right into the oven. Then she slammed the door shut and bolted it. The witch yelled and screamed, but she could not get out and was soon roasted to cinders.

Gretel ran out to the yard and opened Hansel's cage, crying out: "Hansel, we're free! The old witch is dead!"

Hansel jumped out into the yard and they hugged one another and danced about, crying for joy. Then they went into the witch's house where they found sacks and chests full of pearls and gold and precious stones.

"These are much better than pebbles," said Hansel, stuffing the pockets in his jerkin and his knickerbockers with them.

"I'll take some too," said Gretel, and she filled her apron full.

"Now let's get away from here as fast as we can," said Hansel.

When they had wandered a while they came to a river too broad for them to swim across. While they were wondering what to do a white duck came swimming by and Gretel asked it to carry them to the other bank, which it kindly did, taking first Gretel and then Hansel.

On the far side of the river the forest was less thick and the children soon began to see trees and streams that they recognized. At

last they caught sight of their father's house in the distance, and although they were very tired by now, they started to run. They ran all the way home, and straight into their father's arms. The poor man had regretted his act a thousand times over and had grown thin and grey worrying about them. Their evil stepmother, fortunately, had died.

"Look, father, what we've brought home!" cried the children, and they heaped the witch's treasure onto the table so that pearls and precious stones spilled in all directions. From that day onwards all their troubles were over and they lived happily together for many years.

# The Emperor's New Clothes

MANY years ago there lived an Emperor who loved fancy clothes so much that he spent all his money on elegant suits and cloaks. He took no interest in his army or the theatre or in driving through the country, unless it was to show off his new clothes. He had different clothes for every hour of the day and, just as you might say of an important person that he was in council, so it was always said of the Emperor, "He's in the wardrobe."

One day two swindlers arrived in the city. They told everyone that they were weavers and could weave the very finest materials imaginable. Not only were the colours and designs unusually attractive, but the clothes made from these materials were so fine that they were invisible to anyone who wasn't terrifically smart and fit for his job.

"Well!" thought the Emperor. "They must be wonderful clothes. If I wore them I could see which of my statesmen were unfit for their jobs and also be able to tell the clever ones from the stupid. Yes, I must get some of that stuff woven at once." And he paid a large sum of money to the swindlers to make them start work.

The swindlers then made a great fuss about setting up their workshop; they put up looms and pretended to be weaving, but there was no thread on the looms. They demanded the richest silks and finest gold thread, which they promptly hid in their own bags, and then they went on working far into the night at the empty looms.

"I wonder how they're getting on?" the Emperor thought, and then he became rather nervous. He was a bit worried at the idea that a man who was stupid or unfit for his job would not be able to see what was woven. Not that he thought he was no good—oh, no—but all the same, he'd feel happier if someone else had a look at the stuff first.

"I'll send my honest old prime minister to the weavers," he thought, "He's the best one to see the stuff first, for he has plenty of good sense and nobody does his job better than he."

So off went the honest old prime minister to the weavers' workshop, where they were sitting at their empty looms. "Good gracious me!" thought the old man in dismay, "Why, I can't see a thing!" But he was careful not to say so. "Good lord!" he thought, "Is it possible that I'm stupid? I never knew, and I mustn't let anyone else find out. Can it be that I'm unfit for my job? I must on no account admit that I can't see the material."

"Well, what do you think of our work?" asked one of the weavers.

"Oh, it's charming! Exquisite!" said the old minister, peering through his spectacles. "What a pattern and what colouring! I shall certainly praise it to the Emperor!"

The old minister listened carefully as the swindlers gave details of the colours and the design, and repeated it all to the Emperor.

The swindlers now demanded more money, more silk, and more gold thread, to continue the weaving. They stuffed it all into their own pockets and continued to pretend to weave on the empty frames.

By and by the Emperor sent another trusted official to see how the weaving was going on. The same thing happened to him as to the prime minister; he couldn't see

anything but the empty looms. "I know I'm not stupid," thought the man, "So it must be my fine job I'm not fit for. I musn't let anyone know!" And so he praised the material that he couldn't see, and told the Emperor of its charming shades and beautiful design and weave.

Then the Emperor himself said he must see it, and invited all his court to come with him. When they arrived at the workshop they found the cunning swindlers weaving for all they were worth at the empty looms.

"Look! Isn't it magnificent!" all the officials said, feeling sure that the others could see it.

"What's this?" thought the Emperor, "I can't see anything—this is dreadful! Am I stupid? Am I not fit to be Emperor? This is the most awful thing that could happen to me. . . . Oh, it's quite exquisite," he said aloud, "It has our gracious approval." He nodded at the empty loom, for he wasn't going to say that he couldn't see anything. Then all the courtiers nodded and smiled at the empty loom and said, "Yes, it's quite exquisite," and advised him to have some robes made of it, to wear at the grand procession the next week.

"Magnificent!" "Delightful!" "Superb!" were the words of praise that filled the air; everyone was enormously pleased with the cloth. The Emperor bestowed a knighthood on each of the swindlers, with a badge to wear on his lapel, and gave them the title of Imperial Weavers.

On the eve of the grand procession the swindlers sat up all night, with twenty candles burning in their workshop. People watched them from outside, busily finishing off the Emperor's new clothes. They pretended to take the material off the loom, they snipped away at the air importantly with scissors, they stitched away with their needles without thread, and at last they announced, "There! the Emperor's new clothes are finished!"

And when morning came, the Emperor ate his usual hearty breakfast, for he loved

food almost as much as he did clothes, and then, attended by his most noble gentlemen-in-waiting, went in person to the weavers' workshop to be arrayed in his new finery as befitted the great occasion.

"Ah, your imperial majesty!" The two weavers bowed and scraped low in unison as the Emperor made his entrance. "You do us honour!" And the one poised each thumb, each finger daintily aloft as if holding up a confection really too delicate for human handling. "Here, your majesty, are the breeches!" he said almost in awe, while the other went through the same gesturing motions with a fulsome, "And here is the robe! And now the mantle! You can feel they are as light as down; you can hardly tell you have anything on, your majesty—that's the beauty of them."

"Yes, indeed," chorused the gentlemen-in-waiting enthusiastically. But of course they were only fooling themselves and each other, for there was no more to be seen now than there had ever been.

"Will your imperial majesty now graciously take off your clothes?" said the swindlers. "Then we can fit you with the new ones, in front of that big looking glass."

So the gentlemen-in-waiting helped the Emperor out of the clothes he was wearing, upon which the swindlers set about their pretence of dressing him in the new raiment they were supposed to have made. They took their time about it, the Emperor twisting and turning this way and that the while, apparently admiring himself in the ample mirror, the swindlers consulting him and each other without cease as to the cut, set, appearance of each separate item.

"The breeches—not too tight, too loose about the waist? Ah no, I can tell, snug as kidskin," approved the one, with an appraising pat at the Emperor's paunchy stomach. And, "The ruffle, your majesty, a soupçon higher perhaps—so," suggested the other, tweaking at the air about the Emperor's throat. "Gentlemen," the first one at last challenged the bemused courtiers.

"Perfection, would you not say?"

"Goodness! How well they fit your majesty!" they all exclaimed. "What a cut! What colours! How sumptuous!"

The master of ceremonies came in to announce, "The canopy to be carried above your majesty's head is ready and the procession is waiting."

"Tell them I am ready," said the Emperor. Then he turned around once more in front of the glass, to make quite sure that everyone thought he was looking at his fine clothes.

The chamberlains who were to bear the train aloft groped on the floor as if they were picking it up; they walked solemnly and held out their hands, not daring to let it be thought that they couldn't see anything.

The Emperor marched off in the procession, under the grand canopy, and everyone in the streets and at their windows said, "Good gracious! Look at the Emperor's new clothes! They are the finest he's ever had. What a sumptuous train! What a perfect fit!" No one would admit to anyone else that he couldn't see anything, because that would have meant that he wasn't fit for his job or that he was stupid. The Emperor's new clothes were praised by everyone.

"But he hasn't got anything on!" exclaimed a little child. "Hush! what are you saying?" cried the father. The people around him had heard, however, and repeated the child's words in a whisper. Then someone said them a bit louder.

"He hasn't got anything on! There's a little child over there saying he hasn't got anything on!"

"That's right! HE HASN'T GOT ANYTHING ON!" the people all shouted at last. And the Emperor began to feel very uncomfortable and embarrassed, for it seemed to him that the people were right. But his royal upbringing prevented him from running away, and he thought to himself, "I must go through with it now, procession and all." And he drew himself up haughtily, while the chamberlains tripped after him, bearing the train that wasn't there.

# The Three Little Pigs

ONCE upon a time there was an old sow who lived with her three piglets in a large, comfortable, old-fashioned farmyard. The eldest little pig was called Curly, because he had such a curly tail, the second was called Tusker, because he was always rooting around with his nose, and the third one's name was Porker, because he knew exactly where he was going.

Now Curly was a very dirty little pig who

loved nothing better than rolling about in the mud. Tusker was quite an intelligent pig, but he was greedy. As soon as the pigs' food was poured into the trough he would push his two brothers out of the way and snatch the best bits for himself. Porker was a good and thoughtful little pig. His skin was always pink and his manners were excellent. His mother used to say that he would be a prize pig when he grew up.

The little pigs lived happily with their mother in the farmyard until the old sow fell ill. Weaker and weaker she grew until it was obvious she was soon going to die. She called her three sons to her and said to them:

"I am growing so weak and feeble that I know I shall not live long. Then the farmer will give this house where we have lived happily for so long to a new family of pigs, and you will be turned out. You must leave this farmyard and go into the world and build new houses for yourselves there."

So the three little pigs rubbed their snouts up against their mother for the last time and set off into the world to seek their fortunes. Before long, Curly came across a stack of straw and decided to make a house out of it. He found a nice big patch of mud; then he rolled the straw in the mud and built a house with four walls and a roof. It looked just like a mud pie, but Curly liked it that way. He curled up inside it and went to sleep.

As for Tusker, he made his way to the nearest cabbage field. He collected a big bundle of sticks from a nearby wood, and stacked them up to make his house. Then he lined the floor and the roof with the cabbage leaves, and lay down to eat them in comfort.

Porker meanwhile had gone farther than his brothers and found some men at work in a brickyard. He watched them load the newly baked bricks on to waggons and take

them away to build men's houses. In a
corner of the yard was a pile of bricks which
could not be used because they were
chipped. Porker carefully chose the best of
these and carried them off to build his own
house.

When he had finished, he had a nice,
solid little house, just right for a prize pig.

Now the old sow used to tell her sons

about the big, bad wolf who lived in the
woods and was always hungry. He liked
nothing better than a dish of fat, juicy piglet
for his supper. And sure enough, no sooner
had Curly gone to sleep in his new house
than the wolf came knocking at the door.

"Little pig, little pig, let me come in!"
called the wolf.

"Not by the hair of my chinny chin chin!"

squealed Curly in a shrill voice.

"Then I'll huff and I'll puff and I'll blow your house in!" growled the wolf, and he puffed and he huffed, and in no time at all Curly's house of straw had blown away in the wind. He himself managed to escape just in time, and ran as fast as he could to Tusker's house, to seek shelter there.

The wolf, however, had seen where Curly went. Soon he appeared in the cabbage field and knocked at the door of Tusker's house.

"Little pig, little pig, let me come in!" he called.

"Not by the hair of my chinny chin chin!" squealed Tusker. "You're the big, bad wolf and I'll never let you in."

"Then I'll huff and I'll puff and I'll blow your house in!" snarled the wolf, and took a deep breath. He huffed and he puffed and he puffed and he huffed and soon the lighter sticks in Tusker's house began to blow away. Then the wolf gave a few more puffs and blew the whole place to pieces.

By this time the little pigs had realized that the wolf was bound to win and had run off helter-skelter to their brother's home. Porker welcomed them inside and then set about bolting and barring the windows and doors.

He had just finished by the time the wolf reached the brick house and knocked on the door.

"Little pig, little pig, let me come in!" he called.

"Not by the hair of my chinny chin chin. You're the big, bad wolf!" cried Porker.

"Then I'll huff and I'll puff and I'll blow your house in!" howled the wolf, taking an enormous breath. He huffed and he puffed and he puffed and he huffed, and when that didn't work he dashed himself against the brick walls and tried to knock them down.

"Go away!" cried Porker.

"Not till I've eaten you three little pigs for my dinner!" growled the wolf.

But the house was so well built that at last the wolf had to give up and go home.

He slunk away with his head between his shoulders, the way wolves do. He could hear a lot of high-pitched giggling coming from Porker's brick house. "Ti, hi, hi!" Curly went, and "Ha, ha, ha!" Tusker chimed in. Only Porker was thoughtful.

"We haven't seen the last of that wolf yet!" he warned his two brothers.

The following day there was a knock at the door.

"Who is there?" cried Porker through the keyhole.

"It's just the old man from the woods," croaked the wolf, trying to disguise his voice. "There's a field of turnips over there, going to waste. Come with me and we'll dig them up for tomorrow's dinner!"

"I'll meet you there in the morning when I've put my milk out to cool," Porker replied.

But instead, he told his brothers to milk the cow that morning, while he himself set off early to the field. By the time the milk had been put out in the bowls to cool, Porker was safely back in the house, with a sack full of turnips.

"Little pig, are you ready?" called the wolf.

"I've been and come back this half morning!" Porker replied. The wolf went away angrily.

Soon there was another knock at the door.

"Who's there?" asked Porker.

"It's old Nelly, my dear," the wolf cried, "There's a tree full of ripe apples on the hill over there. Come help me pick them!"

"I'll come tomorrow morning when my bread's in the oven," replied Porker.

He got up extra early the next day, and prepared the dough. But he did not wait for it to rise, and told his brothers to put it in the oven for him.

He set off briskly just as day was breaking, to get the apples, for he hoped to be back home again before the wolf. But just as he had climbed on to the highest branch of the tree he caught sight of the wolf below.

"That looks juicy!" said the wolf. Porker wasn't sure whether the wolf was referring to the apples or to himself.

"Yes, I'll throw you one!" he said, and he threw the apple up the hill so far that, while the wolf was loping off to fetch it, he'd jumped down the tree and run home. The wolf returned to his den exhausted. He realized he would need a lot of cunning to catch the three little pigs now. For days he prowled around the house, waiting for Porker to come out.

Sure enough, on market day, which was always a Tuesday, Porker appeared carrying a basket on his arm and trotted off briskly to do his shopping. The wolf settled down to wait for his return.

A few hours later Porker came back from the town with a basket full of shopping and a butter churn under his arm. As he reached the top of the hill above his house he saw the wolf, grew frightened, and crawled inside the churn to hide. But as soon as Porker had got into the churn, it began to roll down the hill, bumping from rock to rock with the little pig squealing and squalling inside it. The wolf, however, thought that this was a strange beast that meant to eat him and he was so terrified that he ran all the way home.

That evening he crept back to the pigs' house, which was shut fast again. The only opening was the chimney for the smoke to escape. Stealthily, the wolf scrambled up on the roof, intending to climb down the chimney. But the little pigs, knowing he wouldn't be satisfied until he had gobbled them all up, had laid their plans.

They had briskly set about making a rich stew with all the vegetables Porker had brought from market. Then they stoked up the fire and set the pot of stew to boil.

Up on the roof the wolf's nose twitched at the delicious aroma and at the prospect of making short work of that extra treat along with those juicy piglets. But as he came sliding down the chimney, Porker took the lid off the pot and the wolf fell straight into the boiling stew, and that was the end of

him. He had ruined the pigs' own supper, but it was well worth it.

After that Tusker and Curly both built themselves new homes of brick next door to their brother's house. They were made of brick all right, but Curly insisted on lining his with mud and Tusker had cabbage leaves for his bedding.

# The Little Matchgirl

IT was New Year's Eve and terribly cold. In the twilight a little flaxen-haired girl walked barefoot in the street. Her feet and legs were blue and numb with cold. So were her hands, holding onto her bag containing boxes of matches that she was selling. She looked sad and downcast, for she had sold no matches all day and she dared not go home, for her father would beat her. The snow began to fall and settled on her flaxen hair, and the rich smell of roast goose floated into the streets from the lighted windows.

She stood by the railing at the corner of the street. It grew colder, and as she looked at her matches the little girl thought, "Dare I strike one?" Then she did, and the spluttering light thrilled and warmed her.

She fancied she was sitting by a warm stove, but as she stretched out her toes towards it the light went out. She struck another match. The cold wall beside her seemed to turn to gauze and she saw a plump goose stuffed with apples and prunes lying on a table elaborately laid for dinner, and the moment it caught her eye it jumped off its large platter and ran straight towards her. But then that light too went out. She struck another.

This time she beheld a great Christmas tree, its lights and bulbs hanging over her head. Presents wrapped in pretty paper and tied with gold and silver ribbons dangled from its branches, and at the very top a spangled fairy twinkled her wand. But as the little matchgirl reached out her hand to the nearest branch, the tree too quickly vanished.

A shooting star fell in the sky. "That's

someone dying," she thought. Her Granny had told her that. Then she struck another match and there, standing in the snow, was her Granny, who had always been kind to her and had died. "Take me with you, Granny!" she cried. She didn't want her Granny to disappear, like the stove and the goose and the tree, so she struck all her remaining matches, one after the other. They flared up, as bright as day.

Her Granny grew tall and beautiful and picked the little girl up in her arms and carried her into heaven, where there was no cold, nor hunger, nor fear.

In the first light of the New Year the little matchgirl was found, frozen to death and smiling, in the corner of the street. "Look how she was trying to keep herself warm," people said, but they didn't know how happily she had gone into the New Year with her Granny.